Blue Planet Mission

Blue Planet Mission

Francisco Villate

2021

English translation:
Marsha Wilke and Emily Crawford-Margison

Book Cover design: Francisco Villate

3rd Edition - 2021

CONTENTS

PROLOGUE

By reading Blue Planet Mission we'll learn to look beyond appearances, to embrace life in all its manifestations, and we'll approach our existence from a different perspective, in this transit in which we, all human beings, are immersed now.

We pass through a threshold of light, and reading this book invites us to wake up, to remember who we are and our purpose in life, and to recognize the presence of other beings who lovingly accompany us, revealing majestic mysteries of the universe within this silent energy which profoundly moves our planet.

To open our hearts and remember is the central message in this book, which tells a story that could well be going on at this very moment, in any of our cities, with characters we come across every day without even noticing them.

Maria Clara Gonzalez De Urbina
October, 2012

1 THE SEARCH

Several months have passed since I left the blue planet and the people I dearly love. My being has grown enormously thanks to my experiences there. I am writing this report today, not for my superiors, but for myself or for someone who may read it one day on Earth. I have learned a lot about the fate of the planet, and I know that few humans know what is ahead and the reason behind it.

With the story I am telling here, I seek to remember everything that happened to me. Should the laws of Creation allow it, perhaps a sleeping human being will awaken and recall his or her true mission on the planet.

Who am I? Well, let's say that I am an inhabitant of the cosmos. I am not like the humans. Few have had the experiences I have gone through. Or, if they have, have forgotten about them. To some, I am an extraterrestrial. This term, however, makes me feel like a stranger. I understand that I am part of everything and of all beings. Today, I feel more human than ever.

In the beginning, I was there, in the big city. My

appearance was that of a poorly clothed youth. I was very lonely despite being surrounded by millions of people who hurriedly drove their cars or walked the streets towards their place of work or study. At all times, I remembered Zitnia, the place where I come from, and the contrast between the two worlds affected me deeply.

"Jendua, you must understand that every world has what it needs," my guide used to tell me before I came down to this planet. "You will see great contrasts on Earth, and you must not think that the terrestrials are unfortunate; they are simply in an environment where they still have learning to do. In spite of material difficulties, in some worlds like this one, the heart may begin to awaken to spiritual riches."

Some terrestrials, surrounded by great luxury, mistakenly feel powerful. Others, lacking the material comforts that few possess, mistakenly feel weak. What affected me most was seeing that, in many of them, the loving light of their inner being did not shine on their chest. Their aura mildly radiated a grayish color, and they had highly conflicting thoughts. Very few understood the true meaning of existence.

They could not understand the purpose of their passage through Earth nor could they imagine what was to come as a consequence of their irresponsible actions. In case they had some insight, they refused to face it and devoted themselves completely to their daily routines. Many did not even look for their guide in their inner being or feel the presence of Creation in every leaf, every tree, every raindrop, every atom of air they breathed, or in the beings that surrounded them. Amid millions of brothers, they felt isolated, separated, lonely… They had a long way to go before expanding their loving light and becoming one with the Universe.

"This is the way it is meant to be," my guide explained. "Learning takes place like this on Earth and similar planets. When you are down there, you might see them as imperfect and unaware of reality and the purpose of their existence. All the same, you should feel their inner being—perfect and pure—radiate love to them, and encourage them to go on. You must look beyond what the third dimension shows you."

And my guide was right. If I observed in the same way as they did, I would only see injustice, pain, selfishness, anxiety, and loneliness. I would suffer depression and be ashamed of it, since depression is a crime in the place where I come from because it only succeeds in radiating conflicting thoughts that prevent aiding other beings and one's self.

And there I was, on that planet, on my new mission.

"Earth is close to a large cosmic change," the mission commander had told me. My guide had said the same to me.

I knew that the change would come very soon, and that beings like me, coming from various planets, were arriving on Earth to help our cosmic brothers. Change is not easy; not all are prepared to face it. The guides said that the time for harvest was near, the point of convergence of many forces from different dimensions, in the same place in the Universe and at the same moment in evolution. Though several beings who had been sent previously remained asleep. It seems incredible that someone who has been traveling across countless worlds, learning and helping, would forget everything upon arriving on Earth.

"Part of your mission is to wake up Zendor, thus helping to awaken others like him," my guide had made it clear. "He was sent many centuries ago and forgot the true purpose of his mission over time. When he awakes, he will help others open their hearts and remember their true identity."

* * *

Water dripped down the walls. A few rats walked on the ground. The tunnel was almost completely dark. However, I was not afraid at all. Mentally, I radiated light to the sewer, imagining a ray beaming from my forehead and filling everything with light. As I did so, it actually happened. There were many sad energies and thoughts there. The children, youths, and adults who lived in the sewers flooded the place with them. By radiating a violet energy around myself, I was able to purify the rarefied air and breathe pure air.

I walked stealthily and felt the presence of three people just around the tunnel ahead: a woman, a boy, and a baby. I only hoped that my disguise would fulfill its purpose.

They observed me fearfully from the moment I arrived. Their aura immediately changed color, and I perceived in their thoughts a memory of "The Rat," the name given to the assassin who roamed the place. These young people of the sewers normally maintain a brotherhood among them. At these depths, under this big city, they feel protected from the cold and the scorn of its inhabitants. But lately, there had been a madman who wandered the sewers, murdering whoever crossed his path. And these three beings thought that I could be that deranged being.

To calm them, I concentrated my mind on thoughts of love and used sound to give this energy more power. I whistled a soft sequence of notes that resonated inside the sewer. The walls began to radiate a pink light, and the air filled with a pleasant aroma of flowers. Though the beings were incapable of perceiving this beautiful concert of lights and vibrations, they did feel this energy of peace and love and calmed down. Their aura turned more stable and harmonious.

I approached and greeted them. I noticed that the baby the lady was cuddling in her arms had a very shiny aura. On his chest, I clearly saw a large radiation and, when I observed his aura, there appeared in my mind images of a beautiful planet full of loving beings near the Pleiades. I understood instantly that he was a very courageous being who had chosen to be born in that hostile environment. Surely, he had a very special mission to accomplish in future years on a renewed Earth.

"Who are you?" asked the woman, still a little concerned about my presence.

"My name is Toto," I said. "I haven't eaten anything today and I'm hungry. Can you give me something to eat?"

She observed me carefully and decided she liked me, so she asked the young friend who accompanied her to give me something from what they had just collected from the garbage above.

I immediately regretted my attempt to seem so natural while asking for something to eat. The young man removed a big piece of foul-smelling fish from a dirty plastic bag and offered it to me. I took only a very small portion and radiated lots of light on it until the bad scent disappeared and its molecular structure changed. Never had I eaten anything like this! After just one bite, and without their noticing, I discarded the rest as fast as I could.

After a brief conversation, I thanked them and went on my way. I felt something of Zendor's vibrations, but it was not easy for me to tell where he was. He had been there, but I did not know when.

That was why I decided to go up to the surface of the street. The sky was somewhat cloudy. People passed by my side, apparently not observing me yet unable to cast from their minds the fearful image caused by my forlorn appearance. I walked to a park and looked for a remote, calm site. I sat among some trees and perceived a very beautiful energy. Oh! If humans could truly feel the high-energy environment created by trees, their cities would have forests instead of buildings, and they would live surrounded by leaves and bark.

I closed my eyes, controlled my breathing, and covered myself with an atmosphere of light. I began to feel Creation's presence in all my surroundings: the leaves of every tree, the atoms of the air I breathed, and the raindrops that floated in the sky and would soon fall on the city. It had been several days since I had communicated with my guide, and I needed his advice.

I felt my third-dimension body lighting up. I was

transformed into light, and matter no longer controlled me. Like a great sphere of energy, I expanded across the entire city, feeling all its inhabitants, the divine presence in each of them, and the love that unites us in this state of consciousness. My mind kept rising even higher. I saw myself in outer space, looking at the ships of the fleet to which I belong, yet I did not stop. I felt I would be able that day to communicate with my spiritual guide in subtle dimensions and, thus, should not try to contact my space fleet companions, but instead keep rising higher and higher.

I saw myself traveling through a tunnel of white light and arriving in a luminous place, full of harmony. There I was, in that dimension, feeling the presence of my guide and observing his face; that is, the image he projects to help me communicate with him. I saw him with his white hair and beard and his beautiful smile.

"How are you, my friend?" he asked.

"Very well," I replied, "but rather sad for having been unable to speak with you recently. As you know, I haven't found Zendor. I only find people with many problems and locked up in dismal places, also prisoners of their fears, anxieties, and material desires."

"You must radiate lots of love to them," said my guide. "That is what we do from these dimensions, but the energy cannot descend completely due to the great armor they have created around the planet and themselves. By being there, in their dimension, you can channel those energies and help raise the vibrational level of their planet, thus allowing a gentler transition towards a new state."

The weather around me began to change while I communicated with my guide. A gentle rain fell on my body. I lost my concentration and had to come back. I awoke in my body and saw myself among the trees, feeling happy for having contacted my guide again. Great joy filled everything around me. I saw how luminous drops of water cleaned the atmosphere. The air turned fresher and purer. After a short while, the rain stopped, and I left the park to go back to the streets and the search for Zendor.

2 A NEW FAMILY

"I don't care what you say. You should have thought about it before!"

"Really? How can you be so unfair to me? Think of all I've done for this family. Is this the way you repay me?"

I listened to this discussion in my mind. I stopped in front of a luxurious house and concentrated on the thoughts that came to me. I went inside with my imagination and saw a couple arguing.

"Will you also blame me again for the death of our son?"

"You did not love him, and he felt it. Your lack of love led him to suicide."

Conflict in that home was very strong. I tried to figure out what had happened. I increased my concentration and visualized some scenes. I saw a blond, very sensitive young man about twenty-two years old: their son. He attended a prestigious university in the city and felt enormous pressure to obtain good grades. By devoting their energy to increasing their material well-being, his parents had neglected to give him affection. The young man thought he could please his parents with good grades and obtain the love he lacked, but he was not doing well at the university. Anxiety blocked his mind, and his fears did not allow him to connect to the wisdom of the Universe. His inability to meet the challenge of being an excellent student led him to become disappointed with life, and he decided to kill himself. What an enormous mistake!

Had the young man understood that love is everywhere and in all of us, had he perceived the deep love that exists in nature and in all beings, had he opened his heart to allow the light of beings from superior planes to enter, perhaps that love would have exceeded that of his parents, and he would have been an upstanding youth. Alas, this had not happened. He did not understand that life is a miracle of Creation and must be respected.

"He must learn from his own experience and will have a new chance to find that path of light and peace," my guide would have said if he had been there.

That home worried me. I knew that this family should also learn by their own experience. Yet I could not be indifferent towards it. I knew I had to contribute in some way. Zendor could wait for a little longer. Perhaps I could assist them quickly and continue with my mission later.

That is why I decided to take on a short additional mission. I was prepared to cooperate with this home. I knew I could not get involved, but I could help. Such is the law of the Universe. Yet how difficult it is to find the subtle line between helping and becoming involved! How could I help without interfering? I hid behind a garden wall, sat in a meditation posture, and was soon filled with light. I invoked the forces of nature and transformed the molecular structure of my body. I changed my face and turned my hair a shade lighter to resemble the university student no longer there. I transformed my clothes until I did not resemble a beggar any more, yet still someone of limited material means. As soon as I was ready, I stood up and walked towards the door.

"Carlos, Carlos, his name was Carlos," I repeated in my mind.

I rang the doorbell, and the mother of the deceased Carlos came to meet me.

"Good morning, ma'am, my name is Luis Carlos. I wash cars in this neighborhood, and I wonder whether you would like me to wash yours."

The lady moved back in a state of confusion. For a moment, she was shaken at seeing someone so similar to her son. She was silent for a moment that seemed an eternity. Finally, she replied in a shaky voice.

"Well...our car really needs a good wash. Yes, I would like you to wash it."

"Thank you, ma'am. Please bring me the hose in your patio. We'll connect it, and I'll wash your car."

She went into the house hastily, still shocked by my appearance. She did not realize that I had no reason for knowing they had a hose on the patio and did not think of confirming whether anyone in the neighborhood knew me.

"Antonio, Antonio, come."

Her husband, still upset by the recent argument, approached her, puzzled.

"What's the matter?"

"A young man wants to wash our car, but..."

"But, what?"

"Better look for yourself."

Intrigued, Antonio went outside. He, too, was surprised when he saw me. For an instant, I saw a pink glow of love in his aura—a rather distorted love due to the pain from the loss of his son. For a brief moment, he thought I was his son, mysteriously returning from the afterlife. But then he felt very distrustful, and his aura turned somewhat darker.

"Who are you? What do you want from us?"

"My name is Luis Carlos," I answered. "I only want to wash your car. That is, if you would like me to."

I gave his eyes a deep look and radiated lots of love to help him. Somewhat uncomfortable, he took a step back. I ceased looking at him, since I did not want to press him too much into accepting my proposal.

He stopped to think for a moment, and when he truly felt he could trust me, he accepted.

"Very well, wash it. Tell me if there's anything you need."

While washing the car, I perceived very strong energies coming from inside it. A lot of pain was impregnated there. The water I was using charged itself with a very shiny violet-colored energy, raising its vibrational level and transforming the pain and sadness into consolation and hope.

If humans could see and feel the energies their thoughts and feelings leave in everything that surrounds them, perhaps they would avoid soiling their environment psychically. Sometimes, I compared beings from third dimension planets, such as Earth, to blind people who throw garbage they cannot see and then suffer from the foul odor and bacteria it produces. It is impossible to avoid or collect garbage if one is unaware of its existence. I did not blame them. Had I chosen to be born in the body of a being of this planet instead of my own temporary one, maybe I would have gone through the same experiences and sorrows. Perhaps I would be as asleep as Zendor.

Antonio came outside with his wife Clara to see how my work was progressing, although they were more interested in who I was than in what I was doing.

"Very well, lad," he said, "Clean this side also."

They fixed their eyes on me, still surprised by my looks. When I finished, they invited me into the house and offered me food. Once again, I had to change the molecular content of food in order to digest it, although this time it was easier.

"And where do you live, Luis Carlos?"

"Temporarily, near the hills, in the squatter neighborhood."

"Do you live alone or with your parents?" she asked.

"I'm all by myself in the city. I have no friends, although I am looking for someone who will soon become one."

They felt an immense desire to embrace me and say, "Welcome home, my son." But they refrained because they knew I was only a mirage arrived from nowhere. Despite my resemblance to their absent son, I was a stranger.

Immediately, I remembered my guide's lessons. He had explained how, in the new state that Earth will reach, all beings will love each other deeply. They will not feel as isolated as they are now, and the pain and poverty of their fellow beings will be experienced as their own. There will be no more beggars or homeless people on the streets. Whoever has something will share it with his fellow beings, and thus the pain will pass. And they will feel as if all earthly beings were their most beloved brothers, their favorite children, or their loving parents. It is a pity that not all the planet's beings are prepared to stay on the new Earth.

"Each one is in the right place," my guide said frequently.

At this point, someone else arrived. "Hello! Is anybody home?" said a beautiful young girl of about eighteen years as she entered the dining room.

When she saw me seated at the table next to her parents, she screamed in horror. They stood up quickly to hold her and prevent her from falling. Her energy was immense and the entire room lit up. I had to close my auric field to prevent her energy discharge from affecting me.

"Andrea, come, sit down. He is Luis Carlos, a boy who came to wash the car. He lives nearby, and we invited him to dinner."

"Who are you? Are you Carlos?"

She looked at me very fearfully. I sent her a beam of green light to balance her body and help her to endure more easily the impact caused by my familiar appearance.

"No, daughter, he is not Carlos. You know that your brother died over a month ago. His name is Luis Carlos. His name and appearance are just a coincidence."

Clara, Andrea's mother, turned to me and said, "Forgive her, young man. Your appearance shocked her greatly. We had a son who passed away some time ago, and he looked very much like you in spite of being somewhat older. We loved him dearly and were greatly affected by his death."

"I'm sorry. I didn't want to upset you," I said. And I was sincere in saying that, as I immediately realized that by resembling their son and attempting to enter their family circle for a short while, I had disturbed them emotionally. I did not know whether my guide approved of me concerning that episode. Despite their disapproval, guides do respect any decision I take and let me learn from the consequences.

"I must go," I said.

I left the house, and Antonio followed me to the garden.

"Luis Carlos, wait. I must pay you for washing the car. And I would like you to come back in three days and wash it again."

"Very well, sir. Thank you very much."

I left them and went on my way, somewhat worried because I did not know whether I had done right or wrong. After a short while, I tried to forget what had happened and walked across the city, trying to feel Zendor's energy on a wall or on a sidewalk or to perceive his thoughts. But still, I did not find anything.

* * *

Again, I found myself meditating and concentrating among the trees. This time, I wanted to speak with the mission commander. It was time to submit my report. I knew that he and my space fellows followed my actions occasionally. It was easy for them. All they had to do to locate me was to give the ship's computer my aura's vibratory pitch. They could then see and listen to whatever happened in my surroundings with their remote projection camera. They monitored me like this at certain intervals to protect me, although nothing guaranteed that I would not encounter problems; only the universal law of cause and effect prevailed over me, and I had to be responsible for my actions. If they knew about a problem in advance, they could dematerialize me and take me back to the ship. However, in a third dimension planet like this one, risks are always difficult to prevent. I felt safer and more protected under my guide's invisible blanket and behind the shield of fortitude provided by continuing with my mission than under the constant gaze of my space friends.

"Hello, Jendua. How are you feeling today?"

"Very well, Commander," I said.

Telepathic communication with my companions from the Space Confederation was easier than with my spiritual guide since, after all, they were at a lower vibrational level.

"We saw what happened in the house you visited. We thought it was very risky."

"I'm sorry," I said.

"Nonetheless," he said, continuing with the message that resounded in my mind, "we considered that something good came about from it. One of our spiritual guides has detected a connection between them and Zendor. We believe that you should return and continue your investigations. They will lead you to him."

It was unbelievable that space technology and the capacity of guides to transcend various space-time dimensions were insufficient when it came to searching for someone like Zendor. Earth's psychic layer, brought about by the dense energy thoughts of its inhabitants, plus the fact that Zendor had strayed from the path laid out, made it almost impossible to locate him. By being there, I served as a bridge for channeling those energies, opening inter-dimensional tunnels and looking in every nook I roamed as if I were a tracking ship. We operate these small, unmanned ships by remote control to investigate primitive places on various planets.

"We have the feeling," my commander continued, "that their daughter Andrea has some sort of contact with Zendor. Check it out."

"I will."

At this point, I heard steps by my side and had to cease telepathic communication with my mother ship. I opened my eyes and saw a dog approaching me with curiosity, sniffing at me, and perhaps looking for something to eat. His fur was rather dull, and the dirt on it made him look sticky; he was a stray dog.

I observed him carefully and felt his energy and the way it was connected to all Creation. I sent him a thought of love. He came closer and sat by my side. I patted him for a few minutes. He felt very comfortable in my presence; I was not a source of fear to him.

* * *

After a long wait of three days, I anxiously returned to the home of the family that was still feeling the pain of the loss of the son. If they could really discover the universal connection that exists among all beings, they would be able to perceive their son Carlos and realize that physical death is just the threshold to another state. Nobody dies in dying.

I arrived hastily at the house with flower-filled gardens. Again, I transformed my external appearance to the one I had created earlier—the one that made me resemble

Carlos. From then on, I kept that appearance.

As I approached the door, I saw Andrea bending towards a flowerbed. She was fixing the garden, which was already showing signs of neglect. There was a bright tone in her beautiful aura, as if she had undergone a transformation. I could see that my presence had effected a change in her.

"Hello!" she said as she stood up and walked towards me. Her smile was very beautiful, her shiny hair reflected a thousand rays from the noon sun, and her green eyes showed a mysterious brilliance.

I observed her for a moment. Her gaze impacted me deeply. Through it, I could almost reach her soul and touch her inner self, gently and sweetly. How beautiful this young girl was! Something in her was familiar to me, very familiar. It was like finding someone who has always been in my memories, someone who has been absent for a long time, yet also a mysterious being who does not reveal her identity. I would inquire about her with my guide, but he would not reveal anything; at least, not at the beginning. He would maintain the same mystery and secretiveness of the green eyes I had before me.

"Hello, Luis Carlos!" her mother greeted me, arriving in the garden and interrupting my moment of inner connection with that beautiful being.

We both stepped out of our dream and observed our outer appearance again. The enchantment of those few seconds vanished but left behind a seed that, over time, would give rise to much concern.

"Hello, ma'am," I said in a shaky voice.

"Please call me Clara. We were expecting you. Come, I want to show you something."

I followed her into the house, with Andrea trailing us. We entered a room with blue walls and a slightly heavy atmosphere. Tension and frustration were everywhere. From the wardrobe, Clara took out a collection of suits and clothes she had selected previously. The clothes had belonged to the late Carlos, and they thought there was no point in keeping them.

"We would like to give you these clothes," said Andrea's mother. "They belonged to Carlos, our recently deceased son. We think they're your size and may be of more use to you than to us."

She offered me a leather jacket to try on. I took it in my hands and felt a strong energy going up my arms, trying to cover my auric field. I controlled it with my mind, and immediately it was transformed into a gentler radiation. The jacket fit me quite well and made me seem less like a young person of limited means, although that did not matter, since my intention was to find Zendor and, through Andrea, I would succeed. My appearance would no longer be important. What mattered now was to preserve the trust the family had placed in me.

"I thank you very much, ma'am. The clothes are very beautiful. I won't feel the cold on the street anymore."

"You must take care of yourself; the place where you live is not very safe," said Andrea while she watched me with her deep, mysterious eyes.

"I know how to protect myself," I replied. "There are tough men out there, but I know how to handle them. I won't awaken their envy by wearing these elegant clothes where they can see me."

"Luis Carlos," said Clara, stopping for a moment. I could feel her doubting whether she should tell me something she wanted to rid her heart of, but her intellect advised caution, since, after all, I was a stranger. Her face already showed a few wrinkles, and in her aura, glints of pain caused by the anguish of days past. Nevertheless, her aura, like Andrea's, looked better than on the day we met. Something had begun to change. This cheered me up because, one way or another, I was helping them get through those bad times.

After a seemingly eternal pause, she said, "Luis Carlos, we wish you well. Take care and be better each day. We want you to know that you have friends here who love you and can help you whenever you need. You may come back frequently to wash the car. You will always find work here. All we ask is that you be honest about everything. We trust you will tell us if anything is wrong or if you require advice from us. And also, that you do not betray the trust we have placed in you."

As I listened to this, I felt as if she were speaking to her son, not to a stranger. Life was giving her a second chance to say what she had never said and to do what she had never done with him. I felt awkward for a moment because I seemed to be more like her son than the stranger who arrived in search of work. There was a great responsibility on my shoulders. Nevertheless, my duty to find Zendor was greater, and sometimes I woke up from that novel-like dream that enveloped me and the young girl who still intrigued me. How beautiful are human beings when they love this way! If only they could extend that love to all humanity...

I kept coming back frequently. Every morning, I would leave my house in the unassuming neighborhood on the hills surrounding that terrestrial city. I had already made some friends in the neighborhood and had never had any problems with anybody. My aura radiated an atmosphere of calm around me, and that was enough to protect to me. Life on this planet smiled on me, but I still had not managed to do what would prevent me from being tied to this place longer. That space creature, born on Earth, had yet to appear.

One day, as I returned to the park and found among the trees the appropriate energies from nature to achieve communication with the higher spiritual levels, I contacted my guide once more. On that occasion, he explained what would happen to Earth in the following years. I had already heard isolated remarks from him, but not the whole story.

He began his explanation by saying that it is necessary first to understand the structure of the galaxy: "The solar system galaxy has two opposite radiation beams that revolve while sending outward bands of energy that raise the vibrational level of the stars it comprises. You know that the stars, the planets, and all the beings in the Universe are expressions of that universal energy, expressions of Creation, or of God, as they call him on Earth. Every being is at a given vibrational level, and the higher he is, the closer he is to God. This is why I recommend that you raise your level of consciousness higher and higher in order to evolve. When the center of the galaxy rotates, the radiation of the opposite bands I mentioned creates a spiral structure. Earth was chosen for its location from among many planets of the galaxy. It was agreed upon in the divine plan to populate the planet with life that could contain the beings who wanted to evolve more quickly when facing the difficulties of inferior dimensions. When rotating, one of the beams approaches the solar system. For this reason, the vibrational level on Earth will increase, and its inhabitants will have to increase theirs. The planet is entering a zone of high radiation, and great changes are taking place. Most of them are not perceived by its inhabitants.

"Due to the bad management of their thoughts, human beings created a climate of low vibrational level energies throughout the planet. They still have not fully understood that individual behavior affects global behavior. They are like the cells of a body—a body that is ill. For centuries, they have been filling the atmosphere that surrounds them with those dense energies.

"As Earth advances towards zones of greater vibration, all the planet's beings will undergo intense acceleration. Those who still remain at that low level will be unable to withstand it, since their body will not be able to contain them any longer, and their spirit will be expelled through inter-dimensional tunnels toward the low-level planets to which they really belong.

"It is very important that the inhabitants of planet Earth fill their hearts with love; it will be the admission ticket to Earth's new dimension. You must radiate the energy that can help some of them to wake up, get to know themselves, remember their mission on the planet, and understand what they must do to help others at this time. But you cannot force them to change; they will have to do it themselves.

"Harvest time is approaching. Crops must be reaped. Earth will suffer various problems, but it is best that I tell you about them later. A global change is important, but it cannot be achieved without inner, personal change. Many beings like Zendor and you must help this happen.

"Humanity is going through the isolation stage," he said to me. "Humans are isolated from the Universe, Creation, and themselves. At its present level of development, the human race mistakenly feels isolated. Humans still do not grasp the connection, invisible to their eyes. Paradoxically, they also live with the false perception of possessing, which is actually a temporary fantasy of the state of consciousness in which they live. They feel like owners of the land they tread; they create borders that exist in their minds more than in the Universe. In their isolation and to fill the emptiness of their solitude, they need to own something. They feel like owners of their relatives, the material forms that surround them, and even of the knowledge they think they acquire. This is a natural step in planets of this type—a necessary step in the learning stage on the way to the new state where they will live more connected to each other.

"Earth is a living organism, just as all the stars in the Universe. Human beings are its cells. If the cells are healthy, the body will be healthy. Further on, humans will understand that violence, power, the desire to obtain more than others, and wars are only manifestations of the solitude they suffer during their search for the support they badly need. As soon as they feel the connection between all the beings of the Universe, they will no longer fight because they will be incapable of inflicting damage on themselves. Since they will be united with each other, loneliness will disappear. A healthy body does not destroy one of its parts. If you are in harmony, your right hand will not assassinate your left hand. Likewise, Earth will arrive at this state of maturity and live in health—cosmic health.

"Today, you can see great changes in the geophysical system, climate changes, warming of the atmosphere, transformations of the ecosystem, social conflicts...these are only symptoms of a temporary disease. Earth, as a living organism, will recover after the period of cleaning and will become healthy. The beings who know how to coexist in the new vibrational state will be part of it."

After the day's lessons were finished, I asked him about Andrea. "I want to know who she is, my friend. Why do I feel that I know her? Have we lived together somewhere else? What is there behind that sweet glance, and what secret does it hide?"

As usual, my guide did not answer my questions directly. "All the answers are inside you, Jendua," he said. "They will emerge in due course. Ripe fruit does not fall from the tree to your hand when you wish, but when it is ready to do so."

3 ZENDOR

The afternoon was coming to an end. I was in a neighborhood where people live humbly, not the neighborhood where I had found a place to live. It was a simple place with simple people—some of them, very special. I was moved by seeing the city's enormous contrasts and imagined that the entire planet Earth was similar, with some people enjoying greater material welfare than others. A huge gap separated this neighborhood from the one in which Andrea and her family lived—the family I now felt so close to in my heart.

The large variety of evolutionary states on this planet truly moved me. They did not depend on social class or other material trivia. Some people had shining auras and radiated a high-level loving energy; some were true teachers with experiences in many places, able to achieve great things; many were still unconscious of their level, mission, and origin. I felt plain and humble in the face of these beings.

Others, however, were less evolved. They had not gone through the same experiences nor had they, at least, made an effort to learn from them.

"They come from different places," my guide had said before I embarked on my mission. "Earth is a place where several forces converge. It is a planet undergoing a process of change. There you will see beings in various evolutionary states, coexisting and learning with each other. Cosmic laws allow this on planets in transition that are about to take an evolutionary leap.

"You will find beings who, in their ignorance, destroy the physical life of other beings. You will see that, in their eagerness for power, they enslave, torment, or cause damage. There are also those who destroy their surroundings and harm the environment. These beings have come from planets where circumstances and actions like these are normal. They are planets at a low evolutionary level where this is the way of coexisting.

"You will also find beings of high evolutionary levels— many higher than yours. They, too, were born on Earth in order to learn. These beings have descended voluntarily to carry out an aid mission, although most of them do not remember where they came from or what they are here for. However, they will be awakening over time.

"A new time is approaching Earth: a dawn where light will cover the whole planet and its inhabitants, a spiritual light that will raise the vibrational level in the direction of love and passive coexistence. Some will awaken before others. The former are the ones who will begin by tilling the new earth so that the seeds of universal love may sprout. Some will not be prepared for this dawn. Having slept for such a long time, the light of the new sunrise will dazzle them, and they will not be able to stay. After the harvest, they will have to be transferred to places suited to their evolution. Only then will it be possible to separate the seeds according to their spiritual development.

"Those beings of great love and wisdom who are still sleeping on Earth and have not remembered their origin and mission will experience great conflict and feel disoriented when coexisting with other harmful beings. Something similar to being in a place where one does not belong. And the actions of the less-evolved beings will be judged as evil.

"My friend," he said, "you must understand that there is no evil in the Universe. What some call evil is only ignorance. If a being destroys the material life of another being or somehow enslaves him, he is ignoring the laws of Creation, and he will suffer a situation equal to the one he has caused. Thus, the being who inflicts harm is ignorant and does not know that, in the end, he is mistreating his own self. If you understand this reality, you will have a lot of freedom. Do not look upon anyone as evil or malevolent. If you regard someone as ignorant or in a process of learning, it will be easier for you to help him, even if simply by your example. Love is the universal energy—the energy of Creation as opposed to that of ignorance.

"Those who hurt other beings do so because this is normal to them in the state of consciousness to which they belong and from which they come. When rejected by Earth's society, they will begin to learn and to raise their individual energy, even if they do not reach the minimum level required to remain on the new Earth.

"Those beings who belong at superior levels will be

reinforcing lessons learned through previous experiences and will also evolve. Everybody learn; everybody evolve.

"You must know, dear friend, that the beings who wish to be on Earth at present are many. These are difficult times, but they allow accelerated learning. There are many, like you, who want to help, either by descending directly or by being born in physical bodies. Not all are allowed to do so. In your case, since you arrived directly from space, you have the advantage of remembering who you are and what you have come to do. Nevertheless, the dangers on Earth are many, and many are the possibilities of being trapped in the third dimension. You must be careful."

During my mission on Earth, I always remembered these words of warning from my guide.

One afternoon, while looking for Zendor in that humble neighborhood, something caught my attention: a young woman was walking among the people. She bore a resemblance to Andrea, but her external appearance made her look different. Her clothes were dirty and torn in places.

With great curiosity, I approached, and, as I saw her from behind, I was able to see her aura clearly and perceive that indeed it was Andrea. What was my friend doing there?

I got even closer and took her by the arm. She startled because she did not expect anything like that to happen.

"Luis Carlos!" she shouted. "What are you doing here?"

"That's what I want to know about you," I answered. "Why are you dressed like that?"

She blushed and was silent for a moment. I saw many confusing images in her mind; she was hiding something.

"I come here often," she replied, and I perceived the truth in her words.

"But why does someone like you come to a place like this? What are you looking for?"

Her beautiful eyes looked at me with infinite sweetness. Her face glowed with disinterested love. Finally, she confessed the purpose of her presence there.

"Luis Carlos, I would like to study a profession in a field closely related to social work. I believe I should prepare myself, and the best way to do so is to learn about the society I wish to help. Like you, there are many people here who have had no opportunities for educating and developing themselves to obtain a better standard of living. There's so much poverty here, and I am sure that that can change. But wishing is not enough; it is necessary to act."

We sat at the edge of a garden to chat. Several people passed by without paying attention to our conversation. She continued with her explanation.

"I've found very valuable people here. Had they had the opportunities that I did, perhaps they would be far better off. Life is very unfair. They suffer a great deal, and nobody seems to care."

"But you do care," I said.

"Somebody has to worry about their precarious situation. You yourself must suffer when you see how little you have and how much other people squander."

I looked at her deep in the eyes, with the desire to address the very wise inner being inside her.

"Andrea, why do you think I suffer? Do you believe that material circumstances are the cause of suffering? I'm happy with what I do. I've seen people here who are very special, and some of them live better than many who have the material amenities that, as you say, life has provided."

"But I suppose you feel bad when you can't find food or a good job," she replied.

"Not really. Although I must admit that I think differently. My personal experience has taught me other things and, therefore, I´m not like others. But I can assure you that the degree of happiness does not depend on economic status. Everything is found within us."

"I wouldn't feel at peace living in a place like that," she said.

"Andrea, peace doesn't exist in one place or another. There are no perfect places, only perfect states of consciousness. Peace is an inner state. Those who achieve peace don't care where they are or where they're going; peace will always accompany them."

She was silent for a moment. She looked at me, perplexed because my words did not seem to come from someone of humble economic status. I could see how her mind was still absorbing the idea she had just received. She observed me and saw the great similarity with her late brother. I saw a strong color in her aura, like a sad memory of his death beginning to surface. I took advantage of the situation to confront that pain. More forcefully, invoking the wisdom of the Universe, and calling for inspiration, I said the following in words that did not seem to be mine.

"My friend, a few months ago, you had no peace of mind due to the death of the being you loved so much and called brother. Had your inner self understood, or at least remembered, that death does not exist and that your brother is now in another dimension but still alive and learning, perhaps you would have had the inner peace you needed to convey to your parents. You are very special, just as your brother was. You spent a long time with him. Through the threshold that separates you, feel the total union that still exists. That loving union is more powerful than the mistaken idea you have of the state you call 'death.' It is important for you to know that you are not alone. We are with you. We all love you and will always be united to you, no matter time or space."

She observed me, petrified, somewhat surprised and simultaneously moved by my words. Even I was surprised at my words. But in saying them, I felt a very large, loving energy covering us. Her eyes welled up, and tears began to roll down her face. Her aura expelled sad energies that now blended with the atmosphere of love that enveloped us. Both energies of light intermingled in a storm of infinite reconciliation.

She hurled herself on my shoulders and embraced me

tightly. She cried intensely, with a mixture of sadness and joy. I deeply felt that beautiful being who embraced me. I invoked the light of Creation, and it surrounded us. Little by little, it appeased her sadness.

"I miss him very much," she whispered forcefully in my ear, sobbing uncontrollably. "I miss him...I miss him."

"Missing him is good, since it is an expression of the love you feel for him," I said, seeking to comfort her with my words. "Don't forget him, for he will always be with you. Feel deeply that he is part of you, even if he is not close by. Send him a thought of peace and love; he can feel it. Don't send him sadness; it does him a lot of harm."

Had anyone near us observed our energy during that moment of inner connection, they would have seen a big ray of light filling part of the city.

We remained there, hugging each other for a long time. Our thoughts united quietly. Without being aware of it yet, I also relieved an old wound inside me. I felt great joy emerging from deep inside my inner self. Who was this beautiful woman? Why did I have such strong feelings for her? I dreaded to think that she could be entangling me in a love affair with third dimension beings. I could not allow that; it would hinder my mission. I did not know then, however, that the feeling was even deeper than that of being in love with a beautiful Earth creature. I feared being in love, but the feeling was stronger than I was, and it attracted me...and I allowed myself to be attracted...

We stood up and walked around in silence, letting the world pass in front of us without making a sound. Everything seemed even more beautiful. All of a sudden, that troubled planet, the one in which I had been trapped in my mission in recent days, now seemed to become a perfect place. Love was everywhere, even in the air we breathed.

She took my hand, and I shuddered. Holding hands, we walked back to her house. Our auras blended in a luminous pink atmosphere and a silent dialogue of light.

Just before reaching the house, she said, "Luis Carlos, please don't say anything about this to my parents. They don't know that I dress like this and frequently go to places they would not approve of."

"Don't worry, my friend. I'll keep the secret," I said reassuringly.

She kissed me on the cheek and walked off. I saw her entering a shed outside the house. Soon, she came out wearing normal clothes and went inside the house.

On my way back, I felt confused and at the same time very happy for all that was happening in my earthly life. That kiss had shaken me and had been like a sedative that made me forget my commander, my guide, and my mission for a few minutes.

* * *

Several days passed. I was trapped between the desire to see my friend again and the need to find Zendor. On various occasions, I felt very anxious in spite of realizing that this was a wrong feeling. I was unloading inappropriate energies into my surroundings with thoughts like these. I sometimes tried, without success, to contact my guide, yet felt uneasy doing so. He could be worried about my allowing those feelings of terrestrial romance. They were very beautiful and pure, but they distracted me from my main purpose. Sometimes I thought that my guide's warnings on the dangers I could face on Earth referred not to physical obstacles, but to emotional and sentimental traps. I knew that a romance at present could be dangerous and make me focus my feelings of love on a single person, leaving out humanity, which I ardently wished to help in these moments of transition. At other times, I fantasized about staying next to the adorable Andrea. Her deep, mysterious eyes cast a spell on me and moved something inside me that I could not fully understand. I was experiencing the feelings inherent to the physical vehicle I had acquired.

And finally, the day arrived when I found Zendor. He was difficult to recognize at first, but I did so by following the instructions given by my superiors from the Space Confederation.

I was coming from the city center that day after taking a fresh look at an area charged with lots of energy produced by dense thoughts. When I got off the bus and walked up a street that climbed to the nearby mountains, I heard some screams. Several boys were fighting. Three of them surrounded an older and stockier man. They were stalking him from all sides trying to knife him. Yet the man in the midst of this aggressive group knew how to defend himself quite well.

I looked at them from a distance. My instructions were to not intervene, although this sometimes required great effort on my part. I simply invoked the light of the cosmos so that it would descend on the group, fill their hearts with universal love, and make them understand that the sons of Creation proper could not hurt each other. The light did descend, but the density of the place made it difficult for it to penetrate the group. The fight went on, and it was difficult to help. I tried to look inside their minds to communicate more directly and give them advice on peace. I observed their auras, barely luminous except for the one of the being in the center and on the verge of losing his life. He had a very shiny aura, and his energy allowed him to foresee the movements of his aggressors and avoid being reached by a knife. I looked inside his mind and immediately saw spaceships. I saw him dressed in a silver suit. He came from space; there was no doubt about it. But I could not understand what he was doing there.

I looked more deeply into his aura to perceive more images from his past. I saw a Space Confederation badge. And then I observed the very strong light radiated by his inner self. As I did, I heard vibrations and sounds. One of them repeated the sound: "Zendor."

I was very moved, yet also worried. I had found him, but he was about to be killed by those boys. Should his physical body pass away, he would ascend to superior planes, the opportunity for his presence on Earth would be lost, and his mission would have failed absolutely.

I was not sure whether anyone from my mother ship was observing me to protect me in case of danger, but I was determined to fling myself at the group and help my elusive friend.

Without further hesitation, I ran towards the group and

shouted, causing the vibration of my voice to disturb their neurons and confuse them.

All of a sudden, I was in the middle of those armed boys who were now trying to hurt me also. I was very scared. One of them stabbed me in the back, and I felt a knife penetrating my body. Zendor gave my aggressor a blow in the chin and knocked him to the ground. I finally managed to control the other two by sending blows with my energy rather than with my body. I was afraid of hurting or harming them. When they realized that now the fight was two on two and that Zendor was stronger than they were, they fled, leaving their partner half-conscious on the ground.

We also moved away. Only when we were out of danger in an alley did I notice a great pain in my back. I touched it with my hand and felt blood oozing out. Pressing hard, I closed the wound with my thoughts and ordered my body to change its molecular structure, thus soothing the injury. Antibodies were resisting any infection that might appear.

Zendor approached me, worried, and asked, "Are you hurt? Let me see what they did to you."

I lifted my torn, blood-stained shirt. Zendor did not see a wound, only my skin stained with blood of a tone less red than that of human blood. He was very surprised.

"It was just a scratch," I said, trying to conceal what had actually happened. "They didn't wound me; they only scraped my skin."

At that instant, I clearly heard in my mind a telepathic

message from my commander. "We are happy that you are well," he said. "It was a close call; we will be more careful next time."

I knew that had the knife reached a vital organ, I may not have been strong enough to cure myself and I surely would not be there.

"This is not important now," I said to my commander. "I found Zendor and will contact you all later with the details."

"I can't believe that they didn't injure you," Zendor said to me while still searching my back for a wound. "I saw how they stuck a knife in you."

I spent some time calming him down and explaining that perhaps they would have killed him had I not intervened.

"Many thanks for your help," he said. "What is your name?"

"Luis Carlos," I answered.

"Well, Luis Carlos, I am very grateful for this. We are now like brothers, although I look like your father due to our age difference. My name is Sergio, but I was nicknamed Serious because I'm not very friendly."

I spent some time observing him. I could not understand how a being who has lived in outer space, traveling from one planet to another on missions of great love and helping Creation in its evolutionary plans, could end up being the person in front of me. He was thirty-three years old and had a face full of wrinkles. His build was stocky, but somewhat haggard at the same time. His foot had been fractured some years back, and, as it never healed completely, he limped slightly. I—a lean youth with fine facial features—contrasted with that being. It was difficult for me to conceal my extraterrestrial appearance, although my disguise had been carefully made.

He invited me to a place where he could get free food and share part of his lunch with me. We arrived at a park where a young girl was waiting for him with some food. From afar, I felt an energy that seemed very familiar to me.

We came closer and—oh, what a surprise!—it was my good friend Andrea. Her eyes shone with joy upon seeing me.

"Luis Carlos, I found you at last!" she said. "Where have you been hiding? I've been looking for you for days."

"I was very busy. I'm sorry," I said.

Her aura radiated a rose-colored light. Right then, I clearly understood that the girl was falling in love with me.

"This friend of yours is a hero," Zendor said to her. "He saved my life. Some wretches tried to rob me of the little money I made working on the street today. He appeared on the scene and helped me fight them."

"Were you also in the fight?" she asked me, worried. "They didn't hurt you, did they?"

"No, of course not. We drove them away without a

problem. Everything is fine now."

Later, my friend told me how she had been helping Zendor; that is, Sergio. He had limited material means, and she brought food to him frequently. It seemed they had developed a good friendship. He loved her very much and wished to protect her like a daughter—a defenseless, intrepid, and sensitive young girl in the midst of a rough environment. No wonder my commander said he had detected some sort of relationship between her and Zendor. It was interesting how circumstances led us to our encounter. My guide always said that nothing happens by chance.

Happy for having found Zendor, the first step of my mission, I returned to the meditation site in the forest. I wanted to listen to my guide again. His words always renewed me.

"I am very ashamed," I said after sharing with him the enthusiasm of our meeting. "I have not spoken to you for several days."

"My friend," he said with his usual smile and infinite love. "I know that you have been worried about your feelings towards Andrea. You should not be ashamed about feeling that love deeply. It is a very beautiful feeling, and it raises your evolutionary level."

"But I have the feeling that if I fall in love, I could get trapped on this planet," I said to him. "I struggle against that feeling, which is strong on Earth and makes me feel quite attached."

"Rather than struggling, Jendua, you should raise it to

the sublime place where it belongs. Whenever you feel your love towards her, feel it very deeply inside yourself. Feel the loving connection to that being. Then perceive that the same union exists with all others."

Soon I saw myself floating above Earth. My guide had taken my mind to outer space, where I observed the beauty and loveliness of this blue planet, fragile and innocent, sailing in the immensity of infinite space. I felt the love my guide had described. I felt all the people in every city, every town, and every island. I felt all those beings, with their hopes, experiences, difficulties, and joys. I was able to feel only a tiny part of the love my guide radiated towards Earth and all Creation. It was a strong feeling of union, as if all the beings on this small planet were my most beloved brothers or my most adored children.

"That love is universal," he said to me. "It is the pure force of Creation that unites all beings beyond time and space. Andrea is only one manifestation of all that greatness. Do not fight your feelings when you are with her. Let them flow and direct them towards all the beings who are part of this place of learning called planet. Control your thoughts, for they create the future that awaits you. There is no consciousness on Earth yet about the effect of the discordant energies of its inhabitants."

At that moment, I observed on the planet a color pattern of the global aura. It was somewhat similar to what we monitored from our ships that orbited Earth. We could predict problems in one place or another, as if it were the weather, but instead of low- or high-pressure systems, we observed low or high psychic energy systems.

Instead of storms, we observed places where wars or great cataclysms and natural disasters could happen.

"Humans still do not understand," my guide continued, "that these disasters are only the natural reaction of the planet, which, as any living organism, becomes ill and rejects whatever harms it. The thoughts of Earth beings either make the planet sick or heal it. They will get to know this reality only when they reach the new state. Only then will they be conscious of the true power of their minds as a collective. In the new state, with the planet at a higher level, those thoughts will also have a strong power. If they do not control all of this, if they do not remove from their minds the selfishness, the desire to control, and the false sensation of isolation, the planet itself will control them. Many planets have arrived at this state, at this point of change. It resembles an exam that must be taken to pass or fail a course. Every human being must elevate his thoughts towards love and peace, for that will be the admission ticket to the soon-to-be-born new Earth."

* * *

The days following my encounter with Zendor were easier for me. I had completed phase one of my mission: I had found him. My friends from the Confederation now knew the vibrational key of his aura and could track him continuously from outer space. It was time for phase two. I would have to awaken him gradually, so that he would remember slowly who he was and what he was doing on Earth. This process could last another seven years. I, however, would remain on Earth only a few months, which would suffice to give him the impetus; he would have to continue on his own. There was the risk that Zendor would refuse to face his mission and prefer to remain asleep. Since this would be his free decision, we could not avoid it. One of the laws we always follow is that of non-intervention. We can advise, but not impose. Fortunately for Earth, there were many who, like Zendor, had a special mission. "Each being has its mission," my friend and spiritual guide said. "All are equally valuable; each one is suited to the capacities possessed in his present stage of evolution."

Waking up Zendor was like waking someone who has been asleep for a long time. He was not able to see all the light of the new day in a single moment. His awakening had to be gradual.

Zendor, or Sergio, as he was called on Earth, told me the story or, at least, the part he remembered of his present life. He had been born in a very poor home. His parents had treated him very badly at times. Unwilling to accept this, at age six, he escaped to the street, where he found other boys in similar conditions. Even though life on the street was very harsh, without a home or a family to protect him, he felt more at ease and protected by the street youths. He lived on the charity of people who saw that he lacked protection and gave him alms to buy food.

With the passage of time, and as he grew up, he faced many difficulties. People did not want to continue helping him in the same manner. Because of his appearance and age, he was unable to find a good job and, at age eleven, he became acquainted with the world of drugs. By using them, he was perhaps seeking to forget the hostile place where he found himself. Planet Earth profoundly affects a being who comes from a world with a great deal of love and harmony. Drugs provided a temporary escape. He knew, however, that by using them, he only managed to damage his body and his mind, and that this would not help him to transform the outside world in any way. At fifteen, he came to the conclusion that he would be safer living in the sewers of the big city. It was not so cold there; it became his home.

He spent many years in the city's underground world, occasionally coming out to look for food. He consumed drugs rather frequently, despite the difficulties involved in getting them, and spent most of the money he obtained to destroy himself with those substances that humans use so wrongly.

After eleven years, it became impossible for the Confederation to continue tracking Zendor from space. When he began to use hallucinogenic drugs, the connection ceased. If humans could really understand the damage caused by those substances, not only physically but psychically, they would not dare to consume them. And if they could only understand the consequences on their destiny of inducing use in others, they would never produce them. Despite how terrible these primitive acts seemed to me, my guide's teachings always suggested that I look at these situations lovingly, with infinite compassion towards those mistaken beings. Sometimes it was difficult to see it that way. Nevertheless, I knew very well that when the day came when I could recognize perfection anywhere in the Universe, in every activity, in every evolutionary level—even in the case of a planet like Earth—this would signal that a transformation was taking place in me and that my union with Creation was becoming stronger.

Zendor spent several years in the sewers. The surface of the city was his workplace; the underground world, his place for nightly rest. He remained there until he was twenty-three years old. Fortunately, and thanks to the support provided to him, he left. Zendor did not remember well who his benefactor was, but, apparently, someone was pulling young people out of the sewers. His words of encouragement and the knowledge that someone cared about his fate made him react. Over time, he abandoned drugs and decided to change.

Although at present he is still asleep and does not remember his original mission, there is fire in his inner self trying to get out—an insight that pushes him towards something very important, in spite of not understanding clearly what it is about.

* * *

It was surprising to see so many people hailing from planets in different evolutionary states and space travelers who had reached the level suitable for traveling around the stars, all of them coexisting on Earth, all unaware of their origin.

Sometimes, it amused me to listen to them talk about extraterrestrial life. Although many had already acknowledged that the Universe must be full of life, not many thought that we space brothers were very close to them. They talked about beings from outer space. If they really looked inside themselves, they would discover their cosmic origin and the fact that the distinction between terrestrial and extraterrestrial makes no sense. They even produced truly spine-chilling films and stories on space beings who invaded Earth. They did not understand that, to a space traveler, actions of violence and slavery towards their cosmic brothers was a very serious transgression of the laws of Creation and would entail the descent of these beings to lower levels where their cosmic power would not cause much damage. Creation's cause and effect law maintains the balance of the whole Universe.

After some time, and without intending to, I met someone else. He was a boy of thirteen who also lived in the humble place I frequently inhabited. His name was Daniel. He was very intelligent and had already detected an extraterrestrial origin in his energy. He had spent much more time than Zendor on Earth and, like Zendor, did not know about his cosmic past.

Daniel became a close friend. We shared many things. His observations on life were very amusing to me. He was an easygoing, practical-minded boy, and he knew how to find helpful people who gave him alms at any given moment. Fortunately, he considered drugs harmful and did not inhale rubber cement to calm his hunger pangs like the street children of his age.

Daniel had black eyes, very beautiful and deep. His hair also was black, and his skin, quite brown.

I once saw him approach a lady to beg for alms. At first, the lady was very serious and ignored him completely, not looking at him nor paying attention to his request.

"Lady, please give me a little coin," he said. "Don't worry if you have no coins. I take bills, checks, and credit cards."

"You should be working, not begging on the street," she said, finally breaking her silence.

"Of course, ma'am. Tell me, where can I find work? You can give me work. I'm good at gardening, washing cars, and polishing shoes."

"I'm under no obligation to find work for you. That is something you must find. Besides, you are only a boy. Where are your parents? You should be at home or at school."

"Lady, I don't know my father. My mother is very far away, and I don't know how to reach her. I haven't found a ladder long enough to go above the clouds. She died two years ago and is now in heaven."

Her face changed drastically. I saw sadness in her aura for the fate of the little boy. There were silent tears in her heart. She took out a coin, gave it to him, and moved away. In her thoughts, I perceived how she cursed this world and this city—both full of injustice. She was a very sensitive woman. Helping the boy would have been better than pitying him. Daniel needed a new mother, and she could perfectly take over this mission. I already knew that further on, in the renewed Earth, children like Daniel would not suffer difficulties like these. There would be more than enough mothers and brothers to take care of them.

From then on, Daniel stayed at my side. He accompanied me often, and I gave him most of the money they paid me at Andrea's house for performing various tasks, such as washing the car, gardening, and several others we enjoyed together. Since I knew how to materialize from universal cosmic energy the things I needed, I had no need for coins or bills.

4 THE AWAKENING

The commander and I defined the strategy to help Zendor remember his remote past and the reason for his presence on Earth. This would take us sixteen weeks. At the end of that period, I would have to return to space; other aid missions were awaiting me elsewhere on Earth.

One day, Zendor, Daniel, Andrea, and I left the city for a day in the country, away from the noise, congestion, and stress of the city. Andrea's parents did not know about her destination or her companions. We headed north towards a nearby dam. The day was splendid, and the sun shone in a very deep, blue sky.

The four of us made up a very unique group. Sergio, the eldest, seemed to be our father. Andrea and I, almost the same age, looked like brother and sister. And young Daniel was like our younger brother. Despite the age differences, we had a hidden, mysterious connection that we would discover later.

We were happy riding in the white car. We rode up a hill towards a higher area. The road was narrow and in bad shape, but we could see other people going in the same direction. They were families on their way to a day in the countryside. The scent of pines and eucalyptuses and the pure mountain air renewed us. This planet was truly beautiful. How fortunate were its inhabitants, and how unaware of the natural energies that surrounded them. Had I lived on this planet, I thought, I would live on mountains like the ones that rose imposing before my eyes.

We reached the upper part of the mountains. A dam had been built there years back, and the lake in front of us revealed all its magnificence. We advanced a little more and entered a forest reserve. The car stopped at the edge of the lake, where Andrea took out several utensils, a small table, and some portable chairs. We laid out a white tablecloth with stars and Sergio lit a fire in a stone stove built especially for tourists.

After lunch, I took a stroll with Andrea in the forest bordering the dam. We walked under some pine trees. The silence was inviting, and we could only hear the sound of a small brook. We sat down facing this stream of pure water. Birds sang in the distance, and the sunlight barely penetrated through the tree branches.

"You have been very distant from me," my friend said.

I observed her deep eyes, the eyes that captivated me. Her hair shone, reflecting a ray of sun that fell on her.

"I'm sorry, Andrea. I moved away on purpose."

"Why?" she asked.

"It's very difficult to explain, my friend. All I can tell you is that I'm afraid."

"Afraid? Why?"

I took a deep breath and looked all around while trying to obtain from the trees the energy of wisdom to say the appropriate words without hurting my friend. After an instant, I simply told her the truth.

"I'm afraid of falling in love with you."

She blushed and turned her face sideways and downwards. We were silent for a moment.

"I'm afraid of loving you too much and then having to leave," I continued. "I won't be here for long, and I don't want you to suffer further on."

She looked at me in astonishment and sadness.

"Leave? Where are you planning to go?" she asked.

"Very far away...very far away."

"And why are you leaving?"

"Andrea, I cannot explain it. I'm here temporarily. I must return to the place where I belong. You won't see me again."

I looked at her directly in the eyes. I radiated a thought of very deep love. She felt my energy and observed me affectionately, not knowing exactly what her heart felt. Sometimes she seemed confused, perhaps even more than I was. She looked at me as if I were a brother, as if I were Carlos, who had passed to another dimension after his "death." I also perceived the strong, beautiful feeling emanating from her, and I felt that she was deeply in love. She liked the way I was, my company, and perhaps the energy projected by my aura—an energy intertwined with hers, although she was unaware of it.

"If you're going away," she said, "we must make the best use of our time together. I want to be your friend and spend more time with you. I want to listen to your voice, your wisdom, and all those things that make me feel so well…but I don't know whether you want that also."

She glanced at me sweetly, her green eyes penetrating my being. Where had I met this beautiful creature? Why did her gaze and her energy seem so familiar? Could it be, as my guide had said, that the fruit was not ripe yet, and that I would not find the answers? I would have to allow them to arrive little by little.

I came closer, surrounded her with my arm, and covered her with my heavy jacket to protect her from the cold.

"My friend, it will be very pleasant to be with you while I can. I love you very much and hope that you find all the good and beautiful things in life that will allow you to evolve."

"I love you, too," she said.

She brought her face close to mine and looked at me very sweetly. We kissed.

Her pink aura grew and surrounded me completely. My

aura blended with hers, and I felt an infinite joy inside me. Our glow filled the place, and the trees felt the energy that flowed from us. The forest was very pleased by our spiritual union, pure and silent.

We stayed there for several minutes, perhaps several hours. Time no longer mattered. I felt deeply in love and allowed my feeling to grow. I imagined that love covered the whole forest, the trees, the mountains, and all the people at the dam on that wonderful day. I felt the entire planet and all its inhabitants. Each being was a life full of experiences. Each one was an entire universe of love.

The afternoon turned a bit cool, so we decided to return. We walked holding hands, breathing the pure air of the place, feeling the dreamy aroma of the forest, and listening to the songs of birds returning to their nests in preparation for the approaching night.

When we arrived back at the edge of the lake, we met Daniel. He was excited and somewhat scared.

"Where were you? We've been looking for you," he said.

"What's the matter?" Andrea asked.

"We've been seeing a mysterious light for the past half hour."

He pointed to the sky, above the mountains. There it was: a stationary, shining light that changed colors. I recognized its energy and knew at once that it was one of our ships.

Zendor was ecstatic. He observed it but could not make out what it was. First, he thought it was an airplane; then, a globe. After some time, he realized it was something out of the ordinary.

The light gradually increased its brightness. Some of the people who were still there also observed it. The ship began to approach, descending towards the center of the lake and hovering about three meters above the surface. It had a silver, lenticular shape, and was simultaneously solid and luminous. My space friends had sent a reconnaissance ship of about twenty meters in diameter. I felt that my space friend Arsion and three other crew members were inside it. They had lowered the energy level of the ship, and it was now visible in third dimension.

Daniel laughed and shouted excitedly.

"Can you see it? Can you see it? There it is. It's beautiful," he said.

Zendor, however, at thirty-three years of age, had never seen anything like it and was petrified.

Some youngsters near us began to feel somewhat panicky, so Arsion, the ship's commander, decided to move away. The ship rose vertically to an altitude of about a thousand meters, where it resembled a luminous point again. It sped up and got lost behind mountains in an instant.

We stayed there for a couple of hours. Daniel retained his enthusiasm, which turned a bit hysterical at times. Andrea was scared but excited. Zendor continued to be silent. Something inside him began to move. A feeling, I perceived, of having wasted time and disappointed someone in the spiritual kingdoms.

We got into the car and went back. I had to drive, since none of the others were able to after such an event. It was already dark, and I drove slowly. I am an expert at driving exploration-type spaceships. I can dodge asteroids or quickly enter a planetary atmosphere plagued by electric storms without my ship being affected, but this terrestrial vehicle was unfamiliar to me and lacked electronic aids and navigation systems.

On the way back, Daniel did not take his eyes off the starry sky, waiting for the ship to reappear. Like my friend Andrea, Zendor remained silent, locked up in his thoughts.

We left Daniel and Zendor near their house, and I continued driving towards Andrea's home. We arrived, and I stopped the car.

"What was that?" my confused friend asked me. "What did we see on the lake?"

"You tell me, what did you see?" I asked her.

"The same as you. It was a UFO, a shiny flying machine, or whatever you want it to be."

"Well, it was only that: a flying machine."

"Who are they?" she asked. "Do you know them?"

I was surprised by her question. Did my friend, per chance, suspect my extraterrestrial origin? Perhaps she suspected something, since everything around me was mysterious. I did not want to go on with the conversation. Better to wait for the event to be digested over time and talk about it later.

"Andrea, let's leave this conversation for another day," I said. "It's late, and your parents must be worried. Get a good rest, and we'll talk tomorrow. I'll see you at the park, at the place where you meet with Sergio."

She accepted. I got out of the car, and she took the wheel and parked in the garage.

That night, I walked from her house to my place of rest. On the way, I was able to listen to the voice of my commander. Everything was going along as planned. The sighting had been part of the strategy. I would have to wait a few days and then talk with Zendor.

The stars shone beautifully in the sky that night. From outer space, I could not see them twinkle as I did from Earth. It was amazing to see so many blinking in the quiet night.

* * *

During the days that followed, young Daniel was closer to me than ever before. The experience on the lake had aroused his curiosity greatly. As the intelligent and inquiring boy he was, he wanted to understand everything having to do with UFOs like the one he had just seen. Andrea, instead, seemed to evade conversation. Perhaps in her inner self, in her subconscious mind, she knew about my extraterrestrial origin and that, sooner or later, I would have to return to space.

I was at the usual park with my three friends. Sergio and Andrea pretended not to be interested in the conversation I was having with young Daniel.

"But where do they come from?" Daniel asked me.

"They come from very far away, from outer space," I replied.

"How do you know that?"

"Well," I said, "I've been studying this for a very long time. It's not the first time I've seen something like this."

"Then was it one of their spaceships?"

"Yes."

"And why didn't they land and talk to us?"

"Don't you think many people would have been scared? Didn't you hear the people around us screaming? It's not normal for a spaceship to land and its occupants to descend and say 'Hi.'"

"Of course not," said Daniel, letting out a peal of laughter, "but they could have waited for the people to leave, and then land. I wasn't afraid."

"I know, Daniel, I know. But Sergio and Andrea were scared."

"No, they weren't. They were only silent."

Andrea approached us and entered the conversation. She asked many questions, some very profound, as if she were questioning an extraterrestrial, although she did not talk openly about her suspicions concerning my origin.

"Why are they here?" she asked me.

I observed her carefully and also noticed that now Zendor was interested in the conversation.

"Well," I replied, "they want to help Earth."

"And why does Earth need help?" she asked once more.

"Earth is in a critical period. It has progressed to the point where its technology can destroy the planet and all life on it."

"If technology can destroy us, and the Space Brothers have advanced technology, wouldn't it be more dangerous that, upon contacting us, they pass on their expertise to someone who could make bad use of it?"

"They don't want to do that," I said to her. "They only want to teach that love can transform an entire planet. If Earth does not vibrate in pure love, its inhabitants will maintain their primitive impulse to destroy. In the end, they will only manage to destroy themselves. All planets arrive at a point where something like that has to happen—a test of sorts. It is the point where technology must be used for the benefit of the race that inhabits them, not for their destruction. If the state of love is reached—the state where we acknowledge that we are sons and daughters of the same Creation—there will be no more conflicts. We will not hurt our brothers even if their skin color or their beliefs, based on their own experience, are different from ours."

"If they really want to help, why don't they introduce themselves publicly? Why don't they come down in front of everybody and explain what you are saying?"

"There's still a bellicose spirit in human nature," I replied to her. "If they descend, Earth beings will most likely think that the space beings are here to invade, damage, or take undue advantage of them. Besides, they are not allowed to intervene. If they interfere directly with human evolution, Earth beings will not learn. The only thing they can do is give advice based on their knowledge and experience."

"How do we know that some extraterrestrials do not come to cause harm? Good and evil are everywhere. I suppose that extraterrestrials may be good or evil, isn't that so?"

I took a deep breath and asked Creation for inspiration. A loving energy covered me, and my aura took on a great brightness. Daniel surely saw something of that luminosity, because he took a step back, stood still, and observed me.

"My friend," I said to Andrea, "good and evil do not exist in the Universe, only wisdom and ignorance. What you call evil is only ignorance of the kind that leads beings into harming others who are part of the same Creation. Beings who are ignorant or are still learning the natural laws remain on planets like Earth and are not allowed to go anywhere else in space. They need to reach higher evolutionary levels to travel and move in space-time. If a being has the capacity to do it, he will have surpassed his present level on Earth. He will have understood natural laws and will not feel isolated. He will be part of everything, part of Creation, and part of all the beings that inhabit the great cosmos."

It is not easy to take anyone from Earth to outer space. Only a few of the planet's inhabitants are capable of being taken there. The level of evolution and love is not sufficient to bring them all aboard one of our ships. We were ready to rescue all of humanity in case of total crisis. But we would not be able to, since only ten percent would have the level of evolution necessary to come to our dimension, and some could be afraid of us. It is not possible to come aboard a fourth dimension ship when you are still in the third dimension. And if you are afraid or do not wish to board, we cannot force you; it is part of the rules.

Our calculations and the lessons of our guides indicated the possibility of a great imbalance of Earth. Its magnetic field—the natural aura that covers it—could enter a radical change and invert its polarity. Should this happen, Earth would have to rotate completely in order to align itself with the sun's magnetic field. And the rotation would increase geologic surface tension, and many earthquakes, collapses, and shifting of tectonic plates would take place. This has already happened several times on the planet, but now there are several thousand million human beings on it.

Additionally, a small asteroid could fall in the Atlantic Ocean, generating gigantic waves that would affect the coastal zones of a large part of Earth. Following the explosion caused by the impact, the atmosphere would be in darkness for several weeks. And there also would be continuous eight-hour-long earthquakes in many places on the planet.

The warming of the atmosphere, due to the increase of carbon dioxide gas by extensive fossil fuel consumption, would lead to large-scale climate disturbances. The level of the oceans would rise several meters. The entire natural ecosystem would be affected.

The mental imbalance of some of Earth's rulers could lead to the outbreak of bloody wars, many with the use of nuclear weapons and other new arms, ready to be used, despite being hidden from humanity. This would make the situation even more critical.

Yet all this could be avoided if the planet's beings who live in continuous discord transformed themselves into beings of peace and love. Earth would change and become a healthy organism with healthy cells; that is, healthy human beings.

For several years, we have had a contingency plan for these disasters. We are capable of evacuating whoever is prepared and willing to accept our invitation to go aboard our ships. However, this always entails several difficulties. It is not easy to make the inhabitants of a planet understand that they are not alone in the Universe, nor that their space companions are concerned about their fate. Earth has been kept in a quarantine of sorts, without any contact with extraterrestrial entities, and allowed to evolve without external interference. But now the moment has arrived when a large amount of knowledge hidden from humanity will be revealed.

On the other hand, Earth's inhabitants are still in a state of bellicosity. It is difficult to descend and say that I come in peace when their inner selves are expecting an invasion or an attack by a superior force. They do not understand that we have been near Earth for many millennia, and that had we wished to invade or destroy Earth, we would not have waited until their technology was developed. Neither do they understand that it is impossible to cause damage without the damage turning back to whoever caused it. And they do not understand that we must not harm a part of a Creation to which we belong. Several times our ships timidly came close to areas with military bases, and they were immediately attacked as if they were a new and more powerful enemy. Human beings even make films that show the supposed atrocities of an extraterrestrial culture. All of this prevents our intentions and our mission on Earth from being known. However, the moment will come when its inhabitants discover that their nightmares and worst enemies are inside themselves, and that they only need the weapon of love to fight them. Only then will their fears vanish.

"They will awaken little by little as Earth raises its evolutionary level," my guide had said to me. "In the dawn of a new state of consciousness, they will recall their extraterrestrial origin and their experiences elsewhere in the Universe. They will understand that their enemies are not behind a border; they are not beyond in outer space nor in another culture, race, religion, or belief. They will understand that the greatest enemy is within themselves. Each will have to fight the battle against the ignorance, fear, hatred, and desire for power and destruction within them. As soon as Love vibrates in each of them, they will understand that neither foreigners, nor extraterrestrials, nor strange ideas exist. Only different experiences and concepts about Creation exist. They will feel the universal union, and their solitude will have disappeared. They will be part of everything, and the Whole will rejoice at the return of the prodigal son."

* * *

I was invited to have dinner at the home of Andrea's parents. Antonio and Clara were very kind to me, and our friendship grew stronger and stronger. The sadness of the death of their son was now disappearing and being transformed into a feeling of wisdom. Problems make human beings wiser.

We were seated around a large dining room table. There were pictures of landscapes on the walls. A small crystal lamp hung from the ceiling, lighting the whole room. The energy radiated was pleasant.

A maid served us dinner; she and a butler were ready to take care of our every need. I felt uncomfortable about being waited on; I wanted to tell them to sit down and have dinner with us. I understood, however, that the customs of the house had to be respected. They called the maid María Lucía, although her true name was Sileana. I heard the latter name as a sound vibration when I observed her aura and also saw a distant image of the time when Sileana lived in Egypt. She had been a very powerful woman, waited upon by many slaves. She knew that humans learned different lessons through new experiences until they reached a state of love vibration high enough not to be reborn in a new life. Sileana had wasted the opportunity to help many slaves and had contributed to the increase of slavery.

The butler, instead, had gone through various experiences in North America, sometimes as a Redskin Indian, others as a cowboy of the American West. It was more difficult for me to discover his past. His aura had been closed by drug use, and he had a dense, gray energy stain on his head. I radiated a love thought to encourage him and to expel the resentment that slowly made him destroy himself by using hallucinogenic substances.

"How are things with you?" asked Antonio, interrupting my thoughts.

"All is well, thank you very much," I replied.

"Do you still live in the hills?" asked his wife Clara.

"Yes, ma'am, I still live there. I think I'll stay there for a couple more months."

"And where will you go after that?"

"Well, to my place of origin. I'm not from here, and I must return to the friends I left back there."

"Where are you from?" she asked again.

Andrea looked at me, smiling cunningly. Sometimes, I noticed she thought I was an angel of sorts who had materialized out of nowhere; at other times, an extraterrestrial. And at still other times, she felt confused, and her mind fantasized, imagining herself married and living with me and a son like Daniel.

"I'm from very far away, ma'am, from a place no one here knows," I said.

There was a long, tense silence. Antonio tried to change the subject because he knew I would not provide any more details regarding myself.

"Why don't we go to the living room and continue our conversation there?" he said.

We all followed him and entered a big room with a white marble floor and columns in the walls that decorated niches with sculptures.

We sat down. They talked about the expensive maintenance of cars, politics, and what the country's leaders had omitted to do or had done badly.

Clara pulled her chair next to mine and started a conversation on her idea of getting work for me at one of her friend's shops.

"I think it's a very good idea that you work there," she said. "They can pay you very well."

As I listened to her, I felt the energy of a message from the Space Confederation in my brain; it was my commander.

"Jendua, it is time for you to advance to the next stage," he said.

"I am sure that my friend Margot will be delighted to have you in her shop..."

"We have detected that Zendor has reached an adequate level..."

"Margot is very kind, and you may be sure of climbing the corporate ladder quickly..."

"We want you to come with us..."

"All you have to do is wait on customers..."

"We spoke with the guides, and they advise that you return to space temporarily..."

"Margot has several stores, and we could look for one close to where you live..."

"Bringing you back for a short time will help the final phase of your mission..."

"She always sells the latest fashions in every shop..."

"We will tell you later where we can pick you up..."

"Are you listening to me?"

After a moment of silence, I quickly replied.

"Yes, sir...excuse me, yes, ma'am. I am listening to you. Unfortunately, I must leave the city for some time. Why don't we discuss the job when I return?"

Andrea, who was paying attention to the conversation, asked me in astonishment, "Are you leaving?"

Again, her deep eyes looked at me carefully. I felt sadness coming out from deep inside her.

"I will only be gone a few days," I said to them. "Don't worry. I'll be back soon."

"And where are you going?" her mother asked.

"I'm going to meet with some friends I haven't seen in a long time. I must leave the city and go very far away."

The three looked at me in amazement. They could not understand how someone as plain and humble as I was—as evidenced by my appearance—had to travel so far away to meet with his friends.

After an hour and a half, I thanked them for dinner and left the house. Andrea saw me out through the garden to the street. A full moon shone in the night sky, its light beaming on my dear friend's face. A magical brightness emerged from her eyes.

"Please come back soon," she said in a sad, faltering tone.

"I will," I said.

I went over to her and hugged her tightly. I surrounded her with my energy, and she felt better.

"This is temporary. I will be back. I still haven't finished what I came to do here."

She felt rather sad because she knew that one day she would cease to see me. Despite accepting this, she kept a faint hope of going somewhere with me in the future.

"You can't come," I said to her.

My remark surprised her. She felt that I was reading her thoughts and looked at me straight in the eyes.

"Who are you?" she asked. "I would give anything to know who you really are."

"So would I," I responded. "I would give anything to know who you are."

I observed her aura, trying to find something in her memories. For a moment, in my imagination, I saw myself wearing a silver suit like the ones we use in space in a beautiful place where the sky shone in pastel shades of pink and violet. There were two suns in the sky, and an endless lake reflected their warm rays. Andrea was at my side. We were looking at each other and feeling the infinite love that united us. In my mind, she was saying to me, "Don't take long. I will miss you very much."

"Don't take long, I will miss you very much," she said, pulling me out of my short-lived dream.

"Come back soon," she repeated. "Please don't forget us."

We kissed, as was usual when saying goodbye. I left silently and, on the way home, I tried to remember the scene I had seen in my imagination. I was sure that Andrea and I had been together on that planet of two suns.

When I arrived home, I sat down to meditate, thus opening the place where my memories were hidden. I had to remember who my beautiful friend was. I breathed deeply and calmed my whole body. A golden energy covered me and filled the room. After a few minutes, I had attained concentration, and I brought to mind the scene on the two-star planet.

I saw myself walking with my friend Andrea. I heard myself calling her by her true name.

"My beloved Jensua, I will always be with you," I said. "No matter the distance, we will always be united."

"Jendua, I hope you can carry out your mission."

I remembered that I was planning a trip to a distant star at the time. There was an important task to be done on a planet inhabited by a primitive culture; its inhabitants needed an "impulse." My friend Arsion and I carried out the mission.

"At the time, you and Jensua were always together," said the voice of my guide.

I saw the bright face and sweet, serene glance of my guide. He had entered my meditation.

"You and she went through experiences together," my guide continued. "You separated temporarily. You, Jendua, went to serve somewhere else. When you returned, you discovered that your friend had decided to be born on a third-dimension planet to devote herself to work like yours. That planet is Earth. Your friend Andrea is Jensua, the being with great affinity with you, and who, in spite of the distance, is always united to you. Now you know who she is. Your wait is over."

Tears of joy rolled down my cheeks. They instantly made me lose my concentration, and I came close to losing communication with my guide.

"My friend," he said, "the reunion of related souls is beautiful. Each of you has learned through several experiences. Now you can be together again. You must understand, however, that your service has not ended, nor has hers."

"What is Jensua's mission?" I asked.

"The same as yours: to help planet Earth during this time of transition. You will be serving from space, and she, from Earth, living like any other human. The union between the external and the internal always creates transformation. You will both build one of the many energy bridges that will help raise the level of vibration and make the change less drastic."

After speaking with my guide and remembering my cosmic friend, I experienced infinite joy. I felt my entire energy filling planet Earth and radiated those loving feelings towards all its inhabitants.

After several hours, I managed to fall asleep. In my dreams, I flew freely with my long-time friend. We rose towards an immense light and remained there—ecstatic—surrounded by the energy of Creation.

5 THE SUPERIOR WORLDS

Once more, I left the city; I was alone. This time I arrived at a smaller lake—circular and surrounded by mountains. Several centuries ago, a meteorite had opened a crater and rainwater had filled the hole. For a long time, the region's natives had held rituals there to salute their gods. Today it was a tourist site, and visitors were unaware of the enormous energy that flowed from there. Our ships use this site to project themselves easily from the fourth to the third dimension. I had an appointment there with my space friends.

I arrived at dusk after walking more than an hour from the place where the public transport left me. I remained at the designated site for several hours, silent, alone, and listening to the sound of insects and the nocturnal atmosphere surrounding me.

Close to midnight, I heard my commander's message. They were ready to pick me up; there were no curious bystanders nearby. A bluish light shone behind the mountain. The glow increased, and an exploration ship appeared. Since my body had descended to the third dimension for my trip to Earth, they had to pick me up in that dimension and thus the ship became visible.

The ship stopped about two hundred meters above my head and then descended to about fifty meters. A beam of green light emerged from its base, covering me completely. We use that energy to cleanse the viruses and bacteria that a third-dimension body could harbor. Then, a beam of violet light covered me, transforming my molecular level. I began to float in the air and gradually ascended towards the ship. A circle of about two meters in diameter dematerialized at the base, and I floated through it. When I arrived at one of the ship's central chambers, the floor materialized again under my feet. I waited there for a few seconds. Arsion came to meet me, and we embraced.

"Welcome home," he said.

After changing into more comfortable clothes, I sat beside the ship's controls, and we took off towards outer space, not before tuning the ship into the fourth dimension, thus disappearing from the eyes and radar of humans. How pleasant it was to find myself again at the love level of the space dimension! I felt all the greatness of Creation. A feeling of solidarity and belonging to a superior Whole filled me. It had been many months since I had perceived that sublime state to which I belonged.

Our small ship approached a mother ship. We entered it and disembarked. Soon after, I met my commander. Arsion left me alone with him in a room with a vaulted ceiling.

"We are preparing the final phase of your mission," my commander said.

We used telepathy for our conversation—the best way to communicate in our dimension.

"Why did you make me come back?" I asked.

"There are several reasons for having you here. The first is to give you a rest. You spent a long time on Earth, and that caused your molecular state to descend. If you stay on Earth for a long time, it will be more difficult for you to join us further on."

We walked about the room. The commander touched the controls on the wall, and an image of Earth appeared immediately. How beautiful the planet looked from space! Oceans and continents and small, white clouds covering the blue planet like cotton balls, with millions of beings living there, an entire ecosystem of cosmic life—an entire living organism of planetary size.

"The second reason," he continued, "is to raise Zendor's level. Should he practice some type of meditation, or maintain a prayer routine, or carry out any kind of spiritual work, he could stay connected with the superior planes and thus receive the wisdom of the cosmos. You will return here in a subtler vibration, and by being close to him, your energy will allow him to reach the necessary state of illumination. Your aura will radiate the energy to ease the transformation. You will have to get closer to Zendor. Furthermore, you already have a psychic connection with him; you can help him contact his guide from here."

"And what about the possibility of bringing him to outer space?" I asked.

"We have been analyzing it. The spiritual guides do not recommend it for now. They envision the possibility of

Zendor expanding his mind and not having to resort to this last resource."

At that point, I remembered my friend Jensua and young Daniel and evoked the day we went to the dam where we sighted one of our ships. Daniel would be pleased to go up with us. My original mission, however, was related to Zendor, not to him.

I also remembered the words of my guide concerning the anxiety suffered by some Earth people by reason of their contact with us. "Some Earth beings wish for extraterrestrial contact," he said. "Nonetheless, the best contact that all beings should yearn for is found within themselves. The road that leads to the place where all answers are found is in each of us. To get to know the Universe and its laws, it is unnecessary to make a trip outwards, but rather to project oneself through an inner trip."

"I have something else to say to you," my commander said, interrupting my memories.

He came closer and observed me with his sweet, wise glance. He continued by saying, "There will be a meeting of the galaxy's Council of Elders. Several of us are going to attend. You have been authorized by the guides, and we would like you to accompany us."

"Are they getting together? For what purpose?"

"This meeting is a very special event that will take place at a point in space-time," he said to me. "We will evaluate the evolution of Earth's inhabitants. The time assigned by Creation to Earth in the third dimension is coming to an end, and the meeting will allow us to assess humanity's progress during the transition stage."

I knew these meetings were attended by the Grand Master of Masters, the spiritual guide who had descended to Earth on several occasions and had changed the destiny of humanity with his lessons of love. I longed to see that wonderful being. I had made contact with him several times during meditation and, on one occasion, had even spoken with him personally."

"Yes," said the commander, who was reading my innermost thoughts, "the Master of Masters will be there."

* * *

Later, I contacted my family from my berth. My parents, who lived in a distant place of the galaxy, listened to their son again. Communication was achieved through particles that leaped across hyperspace, making uninterrupted contact possible. My parents had helped me a great deal during my childhood. As my age was the equivalent of 125 terrestrial years, they considered me very young. However, we measured our level of illumination and experience by our level of learning regarding evolution rather than by our actual age in our present life.

"How are you, my son?"

"Very well, father," I said to him. "The Earth mission is going very well. I'm very happy for having been able to help. You know how difficult it can be to manage planets at the point of transition. A critical stage is approaching. Many remain in a state of ignorance and violence, but we know that this will gradually change. Beings with high evolutionary levels are already being born on the planet, and the transition advances as predicted."

"We're very happy to hear that, son. We only hope that

you take care of yourself and stay in tune with Creation."

My father was advanced in age and was preparing to leave his physical wrapping. He would be going to the superior planes to make an assessment of his growth, and then return. He wanted to come back to the same space colony where he had lived and not venture into inferior dimensions like Earth, where much is learned through service but turns out to be a very hard experience. In those inferior dimensions, the memory of earlier experiences is lost, and there is the sensation of having existed for only a few years. It is like waking up one morning and remembering only what has been experienced that day, with no awareness of previous days. Those who descended to collaborate were very courageous indeed. That is why I admired Jensua, my long-standing friend, so much; she had been very generous in doing so.

At present, I did not want to say anything to my father about my friend. I remember a few childhood occasions when I had. Back then, it seemed to be more the product of the imagination of a young boy than a real memory, and my parents did not pay much attention to my stories. Jensua had been with me during a previous experience when I had another physical body. Now, back on the ship, it was easier for me to remember our past experiences— the events of so very long ago.

I took leave of my father and sent greetings to my mother. In the solitude of my room, my thoughts focused on Jensua. I remembered her beautiful face and deep, shining eyes. I also remembered meeting her before arriving on Earth, and that image blended with the young appearance of her present physical wrapping. There, in the atmosphere of our ship, it was easier to open my mind and to recall what had happened in my remote past beside my friend.

I recollected the time we lived together, united and sharing knowledge and experience on planet Zitnia. We had a son who, after several years, grew and evolved under the lessons he learned there. He left his physical body when still very young, before Jensua and I separated. I did not know where he was or what had become of him. All the same, his memory filled me with peace. I was joined to him in spirit, and despite not being with me, I felt he existed somewhere in the Universe.

It was different with Jensua. I had lost contact. Since she entered Earth and I remained in space, the dimensional difference created an abyss between us. Yet upon finding her again and remembering our spiritual union, the sensation of isolation ceased.

Here in space, the feeling of love for my friend was different. I felt less attached. An infinite peace filled me, and I felt united to Creation with her. I knew, however, that she could be suffering considerable nostalgia for my absence. I sent her thoughts of love to fill the void she could be feeling.

I felt renewed. I was no longer myself. Descending to the third dimension, returning after certain experiences, and finding my friend had transformed me. I was wiser and full of love.

I had to prepare for the meeting of the elders, as we called those immensely wise beings who managed the destinies of the galaxy's worlds. I was enthusiastic about meeting with the Grand Master. Whenever I was with him, something revived inside me. His sole presence gave my spirit an extraordinary impetus.

* * *

Arsion and I were chatting. In our dimension, we use thoughts, not sounds, so we talked telepathically. Voice power is very big; we can destroy or heal a person with it. In the fourth dimension, its power is greater than on Earth, and we take care not to use it, except in the case of a healing process.

"How is Earth?" my friend asked me.

"Energetically, it is a very dense place," I said. "It is a world populated by independent beings. One feels very lonely and more isolated from Creation. And that isolation creates feelings of fear and attachment."

"Oh, dear, what a complicated place!"

"However," I continued, "there are very beautiful people and places. Do you remember the fantasies I told you I had with the girl I felt was part of my being?"

"The one you continually saw in your dreams?"

"Yes, the same one. Well, she's on Earth, and I was able to remember and recognize her after being in contact with her for some time."

"How was that? Was she real? And how did you get to find her on a planet with so many inhabitants?" he asked.

"I believe my guide had something to do with it. I don't think the crossing of our paths was a coincidence. Perhaps her guide helped us also."

"Well, they say that compatible souls maintain a certain magnetism that always allows them to meet again."

"Maybe it was that," I responded.

I made myself a little more comfortable in the chair of

the room where we were talking. It was a circular room with a vaulted ceiling. A table made from a warm and translucent metal floated rigidly in the air between us. The walls gave off a light that made the whole place glow.

"And how are things here?" I asked Arsion.

"Good, everything is well. More ships arrived from Sirius a few days ago. Furthermore, the Green Colony is ready."

"Is it finished?"

"Yes, Jendua. All the bio-fauna has been installed."

The Green Colony is a giant ship that we have in orbit around Venus. Logically, it is in fourth dimension and cannot be detected by terrestrial technology. It contains an ecosystem transplanted from Earth. Little by little, we have brought animals and plants suitable for this new environment. It has mountains with exuberant forests, a salt water lake with dolphins and whales, several rivers, and many other things familiar to humans. Were it necessary to evacuate the planet, we could keep there all the beings we would have collected. Depending on the damage caused to Earth and the time it would take for recovery, the evacuees could stay there for a long or a short time. It would be easier for them to reside in the ecosystem created by us than to remain aboard one of our transport ships. Initially, the Green Colony would be in space for a few years. During the final stage, we would descend towards the surface of the planet and stay there until the planet was habitable once more, and the doors could be opened to repopulate Earth.

Always alert and ready, we monitored the planet daily, observing Earth's psychic field and detecting whatever happened. We even had the capacity to detect the discharge in space-time that anticipated an atomic war weeks before it broke out.

Our universal laws do not allow us to prevent the whole planet from undergoing a catastrophe caused by the lack of responsibility of its inhabitants, but we can diminish its impact and avert irreparable damage. And we can also help the people who are prepared and have a suitable state of consciousness. Those who do wrong must reap the fruit of what they sowed, while those who suffer by their brothers' ignorance can avoid the consequences. It is the latter we can help.

Arsion and I had traveled several lightyears across the galaxy, going from one star to another on missions of aid and investigation. Our state of evolution made it possible to move through hyperspace. When we wanted to travel, by taking a leap in space-time, we raised the vibrational level of our body and our ship with methods similar to the ones used in our meditations and, with the aid of a little technology, we were able to travel across thousands of lightyears in a few hours. Simply put, matter—ours and the ships'—became a thought. Third-dimension beings cannot do that and are restricted to traveling at a maximum speed slower than that of light. At that speed, displacement is not very easy, and what takes us a few hours could take them several thousand years. Thus, the Universe restrains the beings who lack the necessary minimum level of love and prevents them from causing harm. They could be very dangerous in their attempts to conquer worlds, since the only conquest that all the inhabitants of the great cosmos should seek is that of their inner being, and the only enemy they must destroy is the one that dwells in each of them and expresses itself in ignorance, violence, and fear.

Other beings of levels superior to ours no longer require spaceships, spacesuits, and the like. They live in elevated dimensions and can place themselves anywhere in space and time with their thoughts. Their body is pure energy, not third- or fourth-dimension matter. They can descend temporarily to levels like ours and take a physical form. The Grand Master of Masters is one of those beings, and sometimes he descends to planets to offer help through teachings.

"What do they think about us on Earth?" my friend asked me.

"Some," I replied, "blindly believe that we exist. They endow us with the extraordinary powers of angels or gods. They do not understand that we are their older brothers— children of the same Creation. Others believe that we exist, but not near them. They know that the speed of the light cannot be exceeded in the third dimension. Thus, they consider it impossible for us to travel at a greater speed, such as the speed of thought, and reach Earth easily. Others refuse to accept our presence."

I touched several controls on the table to make a three-dimensional image of Earth appear. I pointed at it and continued with my comment.

"As a living organism, this planet has two great forces. Just like human bodies, in which the left and right brain hemispheres are different and sometimes contradictory. One being intellectual; the other, emotional; one, logical; the other, intuitive. Earth has two great forces: philosophy or religion, and science. One is intuitive; the other, logical. Humans separate spiritual subjects from scientific subjects, ignoring that everything is part of the same essence."

"Many religious people," I continued, "uphold their ideas without taking science very seriously. They explain many things through blind faith, without ever pausing to feel the answers in their inner being. They follow strict dogmas without understanding their initial cause.

"Others, such as scientists," I continued, "refuse to accept certain truths hidden to their eyes but clear in their hearts. They do not let intuition guide them. They do not accept what they cannot see nor what they cannot experience with their external senses."

I zoomed in on Earth using the controls on the table. A beautiful take of South America appeared before us. In his mind, my friend Arsion listened enthusiastically to my explanations.

"However," I continued, "this is changing. There are now scientists who mention the concept of God. They have concluded that several physical laws seem to follow the dictates of a 'Universal Wisdom.' At the same time, some religious people have opened themselves more to science and now accept and adapt certain scientific truths to their beliefs. These two great forces, science and religion, will become a single one and, at that moment, Earth will have taken a step towards its maturity. Logic and intuition will be a single manifestation in each of its inhabitants, and every inhabitant will reach the ideal state to advance to the fourth dimension. They will connect to Creation and feel the cosmic, conscious, and universal presence within themselves."

Arsion kept mental silence for a long moment, letting my ideas flow inside him.

I entered my friend Jensua's vibrational key on the controls. The image began to travel and focused on the city where I had lived until a few days ago. A cursor on the screen showed a dot. I zoomed in further and saw her house from the air. Zooming in still further, I saw her sitting in her study, reading. I read the title of the book; the subject was astronomy. I rotated the image to see it from the front.

"She is Jensua," I said to my friend.

He looked at her and said, "She is very beautiful! Her aura is spectacular."

I zoomed in even more until her face occupied the entire field of vision before us, floating on the table. Her eyes shone calmly and moved from side to side as she read the book she was holding. Her image radiated sweetness. Oh, how I loved her!

She felt that thought and my presence nearby. She stood up from her chair and looked out the window. Surely, she hoped to see me arrive through the garden. She stayed there for a long time, contemplating a beautiful sunset, watching the sky and trying to find in the stars a clue for getting closer to me.

"Jensua's mission still isn't clear to me," I said to Arsion, "and I don't know how I fit in. I do know that I will find out little by little. For now, my intuition tells me that we will be together."

* * *

The days following my ascent were devoted to getting prepared. My guide, to whom I felt closer at all times in this dimension, was very supportive. He gave me instructions on how to adapt my body and the energy of my aura for enduring the vibrational level of the Galaxy Council of Elders' meeting.

I toured Earth frequently on one of our exploration ships. Arsion and I traveled over cities, fields, and mountains and performed tasks that were part of our daily routine. We assessed different Earth zones, verified the psychic level of the planet in various regions, and watched its political and military leaders. We perceived the thoughts of many scientists and analyzed the technological level they were attaining. Unfortunately, they used most of their inventions and technological developments to create devices of destruction. They still did not understand that they were only succeeding in accelerating their own destruction.

One day, while traveling over the places I went to when in the big city, we flew over the dam, the one that brought me lovely memories of my friend. Zendor, Andrea (Jensua), and Daniel were there. They had returned to the site once more, in hopes of another sighting.

I tuned our tracking signal to listen to the dialogue between Zendor and my cosmic friend Andrea.

"It's been several days since I heard from him," she said.

"Very strange," added Zendor. "How can he be so far away and not even give you a call? Did he tell you when he expects to come back?"

"No. He only said that he would return. I don't know when, but I know he will. Sometimes, I feel him very close by."

They were sitting on the grass. Not far, Daniel played

with other children.

"What do you feel for him?" Zendor asked. He seemed like a father talking with his daughter about her deepest feelings.

She took a deep breath, looked around, and replied, "I am in love with him; I love him. I feel this is something very deep and spiritual. I've had boyfriends whom I loved very much. But everything is different with him. Sometimes, I think I'm in love with an angel or someone who is not from this planet."

"I hold him in high esteem, too," said Zendor. Sometimes, I feel he is a very good friend. Our ages are different, but I perceive him as a very experienced and wise adult. I also believe he does not belong to this world, and I sense that he will leave and I will never hear from him again."

Andrea felt sad as she listened to Zendor's words.

"I don't know what to do," she said. "At times, I also feel that I will not see him again. I don't know how I can live without having him nearby. It is as if the reason for my existence were very bound to him."

Tears streamed down her face. Zendor came over and embraced her like a father comforting his daughter.

"Why does this happen to me?" she asked. "Why did I lose my brother, and why do I feel that I'm now losing the love of my life?"

Seeing her suffer was sad. Tears streamed down my face, too, and I wished I was down there with my friend.

With my mind, I sent her thoughts of comfort to alleviate her suffering.

"Stop crying," I said in my thoughts, "you know that I am with you at all times despite the distance that separates us."

Instantly, I saw how she let go of Zendor and got on her feet. She looked all around her.

"Did you hear that?" she asked.

"Hear what?" Zendor asked.

"That voice. Didn't you hear that voice?"

"What voice? There's only the two of us. The children are very far, and there's nobody near."

"I was sure it was the voice of Luis Carlos speaking. He told me to stop crying, and that he would always be with me in spite of the distance."

Zendor looked at her in astonishment. He stood up and also looked around. He did not see anything.

I realized then that I had to be very careful about sending thoughts to my friend. She could hear them in spite of being in a different dimension.

"It must have been your imagination, girl," Zendor said. "Come on! It's time to go back."

I saw them move away from the site. They returned to the city.

* * *

I was meditating in my room in the mother ship. It was my daily conversation with my guide. Following his instructions and with his help, I managed to communicate with Zendor. He was sleeping, so it was easier to establish spiritual contact.

In his dreams, we were walking on a beach in front of the ocean. We sat down on the sand. The sunset was very beautiful, and the first stars were making themselves visible. A half-moon shone on us.

"Hello, Zendor!" I greeted him.

Something inside him began to trouble him when he heard the vibration of his name. It sounded like a bell chime, and it startled him.

"My friend," I said, "you have been sleeping for a very long time; the time has come for you to do what you had planned."

"What do I have to do?" he asked.

I got closer and embraced him very affectionately. The sound of waves filled the place.

"Look inside yourself. That's where you'll find the answer."

Then, still in his dreams, I led him to a place above Earth, as if he was in orbit around the planet. His spiritual guide was up there waiting for us and spoke to him about the destiny of humanity. He explained what was going to happen to Earth and showed him the changes that would take place in humanity and the ensuing cataclysms.

"The future is a probability of the present," his guide said. "Whatever is done today affects personal destiny and the destiny of humanity. The prophecies, which were given to humans over the course of many years and which humans with the capacity to see the future have perceived, have sought to bring about a change in humanity. A prophecy does not speak of a great truth about to happen; it is only a warning on what could happen if the present road were followed. It is up to the listener to decide whether to change his destiny.

"It is your mission," he continued, "to help carry out that change in Earth's future. I am and will always be with you to help you achieve that transformation. However, you must change yourself first. Seek your inner development. Look through that path for the answers and teachings that will allow you to be prepared."

In my meditation, I observed how his guide embraced him. I moved away, leaving them alone. I had made the first contact between Zendor and his spiritual guide.

Right then, and while I meditated, I felt sad. Having achieved something very important, perhaps my presence on Earth was no longer needed. Now Zendor would be able to contact his guide and thus continue the transformation necessary for his work. My guide, however, made a comment in the opposite sense.

"You still have not finished what you must do on Earth. You will return following the upcoming Galactic Council meeting. There still are a few things you must conclude down there."

I ended my meditation and walked around my room. I was a bit anxious about the meeting the following day. I also wished to return to Earth. I wanted to be with humans, especially with my friend Jensua.

I recalled what had happened the last time I saw her from our ship. She had heard my voice.

I sat down again and closed my eyes. I felt I was leaving the ship, flying across space and arriving at her house on Earth. She was lying down asleep. I sent her another telepathic message.

"Jensua, wake up. It's me, your friend," I said.

I saw how she moved and awoke. She sat up in her bed and asked, "Is that you, Luis Carlos? Where are you?"

"Yes, it's me. My real name is not Luis Carlos," I answered. "My name is Jendua."

"Jendua?" she asked.

She felt an immense, indescribable joy, an enormous relief and infinite peace. The name resonated forcefully in her subconscious mind.

"Jendua. Your name is beautiful. Where are you? Why can I hear your voice and not see you?"

"I am very far away, but I can talk to you through your mind. I want you to know that I love you very much and will be with you always, in spite of being so far away. I will return soon. Go back to sleep. Get a good rest."

I saw her lie down and fall asleep once more. She was happy. Perhaps she would wake up the next day and remember this as another dream.

* * *

We were ready for the meeting of the Council of Elders. The commander, two female space travel partners, and I were planning to attend. Our partners possessed a high level of spiritual development and frequently helped me communicate with the guides to establish the directives of our aid plan for Earth. We went to the transportation room and entered a translucent dome that began to shine with a white light whose energy filled our bodies. With our minds, we transformed the group into a thought and made the trip. Soon after, we lost sight of the ship's image and found ourselves in a large, well-lit room charged with an atmosphere of indescribable love.

It was an elliptical auditorium with a long, circular table of approximately thirty-three meters in diameter. Several beings were already seated at it. Others were arriving. All were dressed in white tunics, and their aura radiated a translucent, bright violet color. Their hair was luminous and fell on their shoulders; their eyes radiated infinite harmony. I breathed deeply to prepare my body for such an important event.

We were seated behind the elders. Although many of them had a youthful appearance, we called them that on account of their great wisdom.

There were other guests with us; some of them human beings coming from different points in space and time. We were all waiting for the meeting to begin.

The last one to arrive was the Grand Master of Masters. Just before he arrived, the room filled with a very tenuous gold and yellow light. The air smelled of flowers like the ones on Earth. We all kept absolutely quiet. He appeared suddenly, materializing in a chair in front of the table. How beautiful he is! His glance transports us to sublime places in the spiritual kingdom. His sole presence provides an encouraging impulse.

The meeting began with words from the Grand Master. He reminded us of the reason for our presence there.

Several of the elders submitted reports on human evolution. By measuring key Earth factors, they know how humanity is doing on a grand scale. As all living beings, this planet has parameters that speak of its evolutionary level, the one humans influence with their thoughts and actions.

One group mentioned the evacuation plan to the Green Colony and the probability of having to implement it. They spoke about a group of humans who already had been evacuated during natural disasters like avalanches, earthquakes, and hurricanes—a small group, since not all had reached the suitable level. The others, the ones who had passed to the state called death on Earth, would simply keep on renewing themselves in the energy of Creation and getting prepared to go elsewhere in the Universe in accordance with their spiritual development.

There was profound preoccupation in the atmosphere regarding the fate of humanity. We knew that new weapons were being developed and would be used soon. It was not only the danger entailed in these devices of self-destruction of the human race, but also the great amount of low-level psychic energy emitted during the planning, designing, and building processes which made the situation of Earth and its cosmic neighbors more difficult.

The Master of Masters reported that the point of convergence of natural forces had arrived already. From now on, only minimum intervention would be allowed by the forces of Creation. It was now possible to offset the technological devices of destruction, especially the ones taken to reserved places in space. Intervention would prevent damage to the planet from being extreme. Nevertheless, total intervention was not allowed yet, except in case of a grand-scale catastrophe.

Present events signaled that Earth would encounter serious problems in the future. The feeling in the air was similar to that of a father who suffers because of his son's fate—that of a passive son who harms himself through his own actions.

The assembly ended after a while, and several beings began to leave. A detailed evaluation had been performed, and the actions to be carried out had been determined.

The Grand Master of Masters approached us briefly. He smiled and embraced me. As he did so, I felt I was ascending to the infinite. Everything seemed more beautiful and pure. I felt like part of the whole Universe and remained in ecstasy for a moment. Tears of full happiness rolled from my eyes.

I had exchanged a few words with him some time back and had experienced a radical change in my existence. When he embraced me that day, I experienced the same feeling. I would have liked to be with him in his service on Earth, helping him unconditionally, just as I now felt that I had to cooperate in human evolution.

Then, the Grand Master of Masters approached my commander. Together they moved to the other end of the room to talk. My commander had once confessed to me that he had spent time on Earth. He had been born a long time ago on the same planet and at the same time as the Master of Masters. The commander had accompanied him before and had been one of his followers.

When the meeting ended, we were all very pleased. Again, we were transported through time and space towards the ship.

We felt happier and more satisfied upon our return. Our aid mission to Earth was now clearer to us, and we now knew how to steer the support scheme for human evolution. Even more important: we felt transformed.

6 THE RETURN

My whole body hurt. I was in the dark, sitting on the grass. The return to Earth is uncomfortable. It is like being connected to all Creation, in a continuous state of peace, and moving away suddenly and feeling very, very lonely.

"Courage, my brave Jendua," I heard my commander's voice in my mind.

I got up and started to walk in the dim light. A faint glow lit the sky; it was daybreak.

I walked down the mountainside and arrived at the same place close to the lake where I had been picked up. The fresh morning air and the energy of dawn gave me the strength I needed to go on. I listened to the symphony of the birds around me, smelled the aroma of the trees, and felt nature awakening. The sun showed its first rays on the horizon, between the tips of distant mountains.

I was wearing the same clothes I had on when I left for space temporarily. I walked among farms until I found a path. The peasants I encountered greeted me kindly.

Gradually, I got used to the energy state of Earth again. I was back. I knew it would be for a short time. I had to make the most of it.

* * *

"I missed you so much," said my friend while we hugged.

We were at the park where we met regularly.

"I missed you also," I said to her.

We found a place to sit down and talk. She was radiant. Her aura shone more and more with each passing day. I noticed that, just as in Zendor's case, a great transformation had taken place in her.

"I thought about you a lot," she said to me. "I kept dreaming about you. I even thought I heard your voice the day we went to the dam with Sergio and Daniel, as if you were near me, in my heart."

I observed her beautiful face, her smile, and the eyes that expressed the inner happiness rising from her soul. Like me, she felt a spiritual relief. We were together again. We had been separated for a long time, an eternity. However, the moment we saw each other again and felt the closeness, it seemed that no time had passed.

In my memories, I saw myself next to her, walking hand-in-hand along a beautiful beach and contemplating the stars on a distant planet. We were two beings joined in a single spirit. We were two children of Nature, children of Creation.

"And where were you?" she inquired.

She observed me with concern. Although the desire to tell her everything I knew about us burned inside me, I was not authorized to say anything. I would have liked to hug her and help her remember our experiences on that distant location, but I knew that, if I did so, I would cause her many problems. Should she remember those places and times, she could feel like a prisoner on a planet like Earth and become depressed.

"I can't tell you where I was," I replied. "I'd like to, but I can't."

"Why not?" she asked. "Sometimes I think you don't trust me. I'm your friend, but I feel as if I'm not. You've always been very mysterious. You're hiding something, and you won't tell me what it's about."

"Please don't ask me anything else," I begged.

She observed me at great length, feeling sad and confused at the same time. She could not understand why I could not be honest with her. Feelings of love and disappointment mingled inside her—a dangerous mixture.

"And I suppose that you will have to leave soon," she said.

I kept silent.

"And when you leave, I won't know where you are!" she went on.

I did not say a word. I did not know what to answer. I

felt so much love, but I also knew that my mission was very important.

"And I won't know whether you will return someday! Maybe you'll never come back!"

I had to return to space. My work there was important, and I felt a strong desire to help the planet's inhabitants. Earth was in trouble and, upon concluding my mission with Zendor, I would be more useful in space than on Earth. The inhabitants of the planet were many, and I perceived them like millions of Jenduas and Jensuas. There were millions of children, youths, adults, and elderly people, each of them with their own experiences, desires, and hopes. I felt part of that great universal family. I could not forget them.

I observed my friend. Her eyes welled with the tears that her pride tried to smother.

"Andrea, I can't say anything. I had warned you that I would have to leave someday."

She turned her head sideways to avoid looking at me.

"Andrea, I will leave soon. I must go. I will go back to where I belong."

I perceived in her thoughts the sadness that surrounded her. Nevertheless, I was not sure I should say anything to her yet.

"I'm sorry," I said.

After that day, we did not see each other for a long time. It had been a very difficult moment. My love for that being was very strong. Sometimes, I had serious doubts about my mission on Earth and my service to Creation. From time to time, I wanted to abandon everything and live next to my partner. At times, I felt that my love for her was much stronger than I could bear. I also knew that love in the Earth dimension sometimes causes pain after a separation. If I stayed, the time would come when it would be difficult for me to return to space. How I wished to take my beautiful friend to space with me! I knew that would be very difficult. Jensua had a mission on the planet; she knew it deep inside. I could not interfere with it.

At other times, however, I felt that nothing could separate our spirits. Since I could feel the spiritual connection between us despite the distance, separation was easier for me. But my friend's pain caused me discomfort. Her emotional emptiness was difficult to heal, and it affected me.

Today, as I write about my experiences on Earth and recall that moment, I still feel a lot of pain. I write, and my heart cries when I remember that day. How easy it is to hurt without wanting to. I took comfort in the knowledge that I had chosen what was best for my good friend, although she could not understand it yet.

* * *

The days following my return to space were very active with Zendor. I spent long hours with him, seeking perhaps to forget my friend Andrea temporarily. My mental connection with her allowed me to feel her sadness. It was very moving to feel her without being able to interfere with her feelings.

Zendor took a great interest in meditation. I told him that I had been practicing it for a long time, and he expressed his desire to learn about this technique of mental quieting, of opening up the inner world.

He was an exemplary student. I explained in simple words the initial steps of breathing, relaxation, and concentration necessary to reach the state of meditation. Meditation was considered by many to be an Eastern technique. Fortunately, people from all around the world were beginning to practice it, and many were beginning to receive its benefits. We in space practiced something similar, although we gave it a different name. The result was the same: a process of internalization to discover within ourselves the answers to many questions, a technique to achieve inner contact with our wisdom-filled, true identity.

Zendor was quite impatient and wished to learn very quickly. Frequently, I had to stop him and say, "Don't stress yourself. Take it easy. It is more effective to walk in a straight line than to run in circles. Patience is the virtue that allows conquering the world, the inner world."

Several people were puzzled to see how a young person like me scolded an adult like Zendor.

We spent time in various places talking, walking, and meditating together. I invited him to nature sites in parks and mountains where the essence of Nature allowed us to tune into Creation. I often communicated with my guide there. Zendor and I created a very strong energy that radiated to a large area around us and caused small changes that harmonized the inhabitants of the blue planet—Earth.

I remembered Jensua in my meditations. I radiated feelings of strength and love to her and wished she was feeling better. I wanted her to feel my presence in spite of being far away. It was not easy. When I remembered her, I occasionally felt a great wound in my being and a desire to forget her. In this regard, my guide had said, "A wound cannot be covered, only cured. If you cover the wound, it will continue to grow under your skin, and someday it will surface. Do not attempt to forget Jensua; do not try to expel her from your heart. On the contrary, you must keep her deep inside you. Feel the deep love that unites you. You will have to speak with her to heal this wound. The time will come when you can talk to her about yourself and help her remember her cosmic past. It is not time yet; you will know when the time comes."

One day, Zendor and I were in a park surrounded by trees. Following our meditation, he spoke to me about his future plans. We were sitting on the grass, contemplating the natural landscape around us.

"I feel that my life has changed a great deal," he said. "I'm not the same being I used to be. I used to think that I was somebody born in a poor place, suffering the injustices of this world and with no hope. Now I feel that I'm more than that. I feel that my being is eternal and that I am beyond everything I've had to experience. I feel that I must help others who, like me, live locked up in their own limitations or in their own ignorance."

"And how do you plan to help them?" I asked to verify the extent to which he was already receiving the wisdom of the Universe.

"The same way I've been helped," he replied.

He stood up, looked around himself, and said, "We are all asleep. We don't know where we are or what we're here for. We walk on the path of life getting entangled with the obstacles on the road, the ones that our greed, resentment, and lack of love place in front of us. Only by awakening will we know who we are. We are awake when we acknowledge that difficulties teach us as much as success. It is not a bad thing to have problems; what is bad is not to learn from them. We do not learn when we're asleep."

"Do you think that others can also wake up?" I asked.

"I awoke, and I believe that others can, too. I was able to look inside myself and, when I did so, I discovered a very special somebody. We are all like very shiny stars that have fallen to Earth. It's just that we forgot that our nature is bright and that our role is to shine. Over time, we allowed the sludge of our routines and materialism to darken our true spirit. We shine when we're simply happy with life's simple things. And life is a gift not to be wasted. We waste it when we are asleep, letting it pass by in front of us.

"Life is a road," he continued. "Sometimes we wish to reach a goal without realizing that the road is more important than the goals. The road is long and full of different experiences; the goal is only a fleeting moment that gets lost in the memory of the past."

I saw in his mind scenes from his youth and his experiences of recent years. He continued by saying, "For a long time, I craved money, luxury, and many other things that were not given to me. Now I know that I wanted these things to do good to others. There has always been a noble feeling deep inside me. Then I discovered that I wanted to do all those things to become someone special. Today I understand that 'being' is more important than 'doing' or 'having.'"

He made a pause, and I took advantage of it to continue with my questions.

"Sergio, my friend, who do you want to be?"

"I want to be myself. I discovered that I am not who I thought I was. And I know that tomorrow I will discover that I am not the one I believe myself to be today. This is a process of continuous learning. I must change myself before I try to change the world. The greatest revolution takes place within each one of us; it then extends towards the infinite in a natural way."

I could clearly see the thoughts in Zendor's mind. He now remembered something about his remote past in the stars and the aid mission he had set out to accomplish on Earth. Yet he was very cautious and did not tell me about it or, at least, not in all its detail. I was now his best friend and confidant, but even so, he did not feel at ease telling me what he was discovering. In spiritual development, discretion is the best shield against adversity.

* * *

A couple of months went by. I did not see Jensua during that time. In my mind, I knew she was calmer, although still somewhat sad. She had not returned to the park nor to the place where she helped the beggars. I knew she was taking a break and would later resume her aid mission to the needy.

I spent most of my time with my friend Zendor. He talked with people, especially those with serious problems who inhabited the underground sewers or roamed the streets but were imprisoned by their resentment and rancor towards society. Zendor provided them with a different view on life.

Daniel, the inquiring boy, always accompanied us. We were the three most dissimilar friends in the city: a boy, a youth, and an adult—a unique team.

We found various kinds of people in the streets, some of them living in extreme poverty and locked inside the invisible and destructive shield of drugs. Zendor talked with adults, I, with young people, and Daniel looked for children his age. Our task was not to give advice or try to transform people. No one achieves this without a sincere desire for change, and this desire is fulfilled by seeking inside, having the courage to strip the pain and face it, and forgiving others and oneself. All we could do was give a lot of love and allow people to express those feelings.

This stage of the planet was very interesting to me. I saw very special people for whom the lack of affection and love had closed the doors of that wonderful place, deep inside each person, that is inhabited by happiness. I saw mistaken people, people alien to that reality, people who did not give themselves a new opportunity, who did not seek help in celestial kingdoms, or who did not offer that aid to their fellow planetary travelers.

In some people, I saw an inner change beginning to surface, something similar to the first sprouts of the seed of universal love.

Newscasts generally show negative events; they forget that good is always alongside ignorance, establishing the balance of nature at this evolutionary level.

Some journalists, however, were concerned with seeking a different facet. One day, reporters of a local news show arrived at the site where we were talking with several street dwellers. I quickly hid to avoid being caught by their cameras; I could not allow myself to be seen in public. They interviewed Zendor and Daniel.

"Excuse us, sir," the cameraman said to Zendor. "We know that you walk the streets in your personal mission of aiding beggars. We would like to ask you a few questions."

Zendor stopped and faced the camera.

"Go right ahead," he said.

"Many people talk about you. You are described as the Quixote of the garbage dumps. What are you looking for here? Do you wish to lift all beggars out of poverty?"

"Lack of love is the greatest poverty there is. There are very poor people who need lots of help, and if they want to get it, I will help them find it on their own. And I am not referring specifically to the ones who inhabit this place. I'm talking of all those who have not understood that the greatest wealth is within ourselves and that it is there where we can find the tracks to guide us on the path of love."

"Are you also referring to the people who have lots of money but lack love?"

"Yes, to them also. Some seek satisfaction in material comforts. They make lots of money and then require many bodyguards. These people need a lot of help to solve their countless problems. We must return to innocence and simplicity. We are not owners of anything. Nothing belongs to us. We are part of nature, which takes care of us in spite of the difficulties we cause it. But nature will not be able to put up with our ingratitude much longer. All human beings are part of nature. We cannot continue to cause damage to ourselves as when we damage our brother and our Mother Earth. We must understand that the only enemy is found inside ourselves. I look for people brave enough to face it."

"And you," they asked, "are you planning to fight that battle? What weapon do you have to offer?"

"Only one: my love and my feeling of solidarity. I'm already fighting. This is why I recognize my true enemy. I used to blame everyone around for what happened to me. Today, now that I am defeating that enemy, I understand that he was hidden inside me. I'm getting rid of the violence in my heart, and I will cease to be violent towards myself or others. I declare myself a soldier of peace."

Following that interview, Zendor's fame increased even further. To some, he seemed a funny character or a lunatic who wanted to change the world. After talking to him and making his acquaintance, others considered him very special. The fact of having had a difficult, underprivileged past gave more credibility to his words. This was the life that Zendor had chosen for himself.

* * *

Clouds covered the sky, their gray atmosphere turning us somewhat melancholic. We were at the dam again, but this time the feeling was different. Andrea was with us. She had told Sergio that she did not want to see me again, yet felt compelled to go at his insistence. Daniel also was there.

Andrea avoided looking at me and felt annoyed when I spoke. She still loved me deeply, and, strangely enough, this caused her pain.

"In planets of the third dimension," my guide had told me, "love is sometimes expressed through attachment. Fathers and mothers feel they are the owners of their children, as if they were a possession granted by life and not a temporary opportunity to serve and help other beings grow. Some suffer when their children must leave home to another city or country or to transcend to other states. On Earth, love between couples is considered very important. But it is also seen sometimes as a form of possession, the partners considering that they belong to each other. Consequently, if a partner wishes to leave, this causes much pain. If they find somebody with whom they can share their life and believe it to be ideal love, they suffer when they do not manage to keep physically close. They do not understand that love extends beyond the borders of space and time. When united to Creation, the pain caused by the apparent solitude will disappear, and they will feel joined to all of nature's beings. They will feel a total and continuous union."

Daniel, the inquiring, noble boy, approached me and said, "We have come here several times but haven't seen the spaceship again."

"It doesn't appear when one wishes it, but when it is necessary," I said. "Its appearance makes those who have gone through this experience restless; the world looks different."

Zendor and I exchanged glances. He knew I was referring to him. In his case, that had been the main reason for the sighting.

"Do you think they'll let themselves be seen again?"

"I don't know, Daniel. I don't know."

"I'd like to board their ship and tour the stars."

"That would be wonderful," I said.

Andrea, who was listening to us without being noticed, entered the conversation. There was bitterness in her words.

"Why wonderful?" she asked. "Is it really important to go to space? Are extraterrestrials important?"

I did not respond. I only observed her with sweetness and understanding.

"We don't know who they are," she went on. "They hide; they are very mysterious. No good can be expected from someone as mysterious as them."

Zendor approached us and gently said to my friend, "They, the extraterrestrials, are simply beings of the cosmos. They are beings like you, Luis Carlos, Daniel, or me. There's no mystery in this. It's just that they have lived more experiences than we have, and for that reason, have reached higher levels in technology and spiritual growth. They are as special as you are."

"And you, Andrea," I added to the words of my cosmic friend, "are very special. You wouldn't need to observe a ship or board it to arrive at the stars. You shine on your own. You already are a luminous star..."

She became infuriated and stood up and moved away from us. That mix of love and disappointment was a strange feeling.

Zendor came to my side and embraced me. "Be patient," he said. "She loves you very much."

Zendor did not know that I would be leaving soon. I still had not told him. Yet, because our friendship had reached a deep level of disinterested love, I knew he would not feel bad about my departure. The day of our separation, we would wish each other luck and go our different ways, just like a father and son.

After a few minutes, I approached my friend. She was sitting at the brook's edge. The sound of the water carried the thousands of teardrops she did not want to let out. She was absorbed in her own thoughts.

"May I come closer?" I asked.

She looked at me. She was silent for a moment that seemed an eternity. Finally, she said, "If you want to."

I sat down beside her and we contemplated the surrounding landscape. Several pines covered us with their thick foliage. It was colder than on other occasions.

"It's odd," she said. "We were here together. It was a very special day for me."

"Yes, I also remember that day. It was very beautiful," I said. "I remember that I didn't want to see you again, yet I also wanted to be with you. I was afraid of falling in love with you."

"And it was I who fell in love!" she replied. "I should have respected your wish to keep away from me."

I breathed deeply, feeling the aroma of the moist forest and the pure air.

"Andrea, I told you then that I would have to leave soon. You wanted to be with me during the short time we had left."

She sighed and said, "Yes, you're right. I accepted the conditions. It's just that at the time I didn't think it would be so painful."

I rose and sat facing her. I looked at her in the eyes. She was unable to take her gaze away from mine.

"My friend," I said. "You knew that I would have to go. The people in your life will always come and go when it's time."

"Like my brother, right?"

"Exactly. You must understand that everything in the world of appearances is ephemeral. You can see how plants live and then die; day dies when night arrives. Clouds pass, go away, and do not return; the beings we love must leave someday. Everything seems to disappear. Nonetheless, in the real world, the one that is clear to your heart but not to your eyes, everything is eternally changing and transforming, everything is evolving."

I made a pause. I saw a sparkle of hope in her deep, transparent eyes—the eyes that show the inner beauty that flows from the most intimate part of a being—and I continued.

"You're sad because I must go. You must understand that although our friendship and our love apparently will come to an end, I will always be with you in the real world. I will be within you; and you, within me. We're cosmic siblings of the kind that cannot separate even if they try. In spite of going very far away, I will be always with you. It will be enough for you to think about me, to feel the pure air, the love of people, or the beauty and power of nature for me to be in you. If you feel sad or lonely or must face any difficulty, simply think about me; I will be in your heart, and my thoughts will be next to yours. Feel that I'm a very special someone. I'm special because I'm part of you, and because we're both part of Creation, that universal energy unites us. It is more powerful than any barrier you may want to set up in your mind."

I saw her eyes beginning to well with tears. We embraced as we had done before.

"I'm sorry," she said. "I moved away when I should have been closer to you."

"I am always with you and always will be. It may be that in the future you will no longer see me at your side, but I'll actually be closer when this happens."

She let go of me for a moment. She wiped the tears from her face and looked at me directly in the eyes. I felt her energy entering my mind and searching for the answers to her questions.

"Aren't you ever going to tell me who you are? You are not Luis Carlos. Your resemblance to him is only a façade. Your appearance is humble, yet within you, there is great wisdom that few have. Sometimes, I think you aren't even human."

I turned around and took a few steps. Andrea stood up, too, and watched me. I observed the whole place. I breathed and tried to perceive in nature some secret message that would let me know whether I had to confess or not my origin and my purpose on Earth. A very strong insight told me that I had to say something. I had to open the door slightly and allow her to begin taking in the truth.

"Andrea," I responded. "You're right in many of the things you say about me. I must tell you that today I feel more human than ever. I'm a being just like any other. Don't see great differences, which, in fact, do not exist."

I went towards her and looked at her directly in the eyes.

"I come from very far away. I come from outer space. My space friends are always watching me, just as they're doing right now."

She dropped to her feet and sat on the pine needles, which formed a soft mattress. She kept silent while meditating on what I had just said. Any other person would have thought that I was out of my mind. She, however, had already seen and experienced so many strange things that this did not surprise her.

"And where did you leave your spaceship?" she asked with a certain nervousness.

"It's orbiting Earth," I responded while smiling at her.

"What planet are you from? How is it out there?"

"I am a being of the Cosmos. We have no divisions or boundaries there, and we coexist in peace and harmony. We are all part of the same brotherhood."

Anyone who happened to pass by would have been surprised by the content of our conversation. It was not exactly about an everyday subject.

"May I go and visit you?"

"You will one day," I answered. "You must be prepared for that. It won't be easy in the beginning, but it's even more difficult to return; you may not want to."

She stood up again. She looked at me and asked, "What is your name? At least, I must know your name, spaceman."

"Jendua, my name is Jendua."

She took two steps backwards. The sound of the name intrigued her.

"Jendua? I've heard that name before," she said.

She began to remember. I saw images of distant

memories opening up in her mind.

"It was in a dream. Of course, now I remember. You and I were walking on a beach. It was the loveliest dream I had ever had. I felt happy for being with you. In the dream, I called you by that name. You were Jendua."

I came closer to my friend. I stretched my hands towards her. She looked at me and embraced me tightly.

"It was you, it was you," she said, "it has always been you."

We stood there, embracing. Silently, the forest rejoiced at our union. The trees greeted us with the mute song of air running through their branches. Our energy filled the entire place. Once again, we were a single being. We had reunited. We were very far from home...it was another place...another atmosphere...another time...the same love.

"I will always be with you," I said. "My love will always be with you."

At that precise moment, the sun's rays penetrated the branches and the forest lit up. The day had been transformed.

* * *

The days before my return were very happy. Jensua was my friend again, and we spent all our time talking about space and human evolution. She wanted to know more and more. I had to be cautious, however, and give her information little by little.

An accelerated transformation was taking place in my friend. Like Zendor, she was waking up and realizing the reason for her presence on the planet. She already knew of her cosmic origin and was beginning to remember some of the places in space where we had lived together. She had often felt disoriented in her present life, as if she did not belong to the world. She could not understand why certain violent acts occurred. She wanted to "get off the planet" and go somewhere else. But she had not been aware of the reason for this. Now she understood why she had felt that way. We were a couple speaking of life on other planets and in different evolutionary stages.

My guide explained more clearly what was happening with Jensua and the reason for my presence there.

"My friend," he said, "part of your mission was to awaken Zendor. That was the main reason for our suggestion that you go to Earth. There was, however, a hidden mission we knew you could accomplish. It was about waking yourself up. Now you remember your friend Jensua, and she remembers you. You two can continue helping the planet and making the transition to the new state easier. Jensua decided to be born on Earth and to prepare herself for this moment. She has been under different lives and teachings for several centuries. You have received instructions in space regarding visits to different worlds. Through various experiences, you both acquired profound knowledge on how to help humanity effectively. You must understand that you are not unique. Like you two, there are many beings on Earth carrying out similar tasks. You have the great advantage of being awake and aware of what you are doing and of doing your work from two extremes—the inner and the outer—that are joined by means of the bridge of light that has been created already. You are now a bridge between the cosmic and the terrestrial.

"When you return to space," he said, "you will be able to maintain telepathic communication with your friend. You will be capable of guiding her and learning from her experiences on Earth. With Zendor, she will be striving for the awakening of all humanity's beings. The day will arrive when everything that should be known will be known on the surface of Earth. There are, nonetheless, difficult days ahead for its inhabitants. Deep and sincere love will be the shield that protects them from adversity. It is all part of a process of transformation.

"Very soon," he said, "time will be perceived differently. Time in the third dimension is a straight line, with a remote past and an uncertain future. As perceived in the space dimension, the new state is a plane where the central point is the most important. Earth beings will feel a continuous present. The past will not be distant nor the future uncertain. A gradual change in time is now taking place. Human beings feel that each day passes faster, years seem shorter, and days become ephemeral. This is a natural process. The day when time becomes null, they will have passed to the fourth dimension. At that moment, the level of consciousness will be greater, and they will feel connected to each other in a continuous and present instant of inner happiness."

* * *

"So, are you leaving?" my friend Zendor asked.

"Yes, Sergio, I must leave now."

"I'm going to miss you," he said. "You have been like a son and a father to me, and you have taught me beautiful things."

"Thank you. I will be thinking about you," I said to him.

"I hope you find marvelous things at the place where you're going. You are someone special, and I know that you will effect great changes in others."

Zendor did not know—at least, not consciously—that I am not human. I was not allowed to reveal this to him.

"Since you arrived," he continued, "my life changed completely. You arrived like an angel fallen from the sky. I want you to know that you will always be my friend."

I threw myself at him and embraced him tightly. I felt very happy about having made Zendor's acquaintance. I admired him for his immense courage in deciding to come down to worlds like this and coexist with their difficulties. I also knew he would now have to face other types of tests during the course of his work. When a change is attempted, resistance always arises; he would have to confront it.

That same day, I went to Andrea's house and said goodbye to her parents and the household help. They had all been very kind to me and made me feel like a member of the family.

It was easy to say goodbye to them. With my young friend Daniel, however, it was more complicated. As I said goodbye, I remembered the difficulties that would befall Earth. I felt he was so defenseless in a primitive world. I wanted to take him with me right then. I also wanted to take all the world's children to space. My comfort was in knowing that, in case of a total emergency on the blue planet, and should an evacuation be required, the children would be the first saved.

"Don't go, please," he said while he cried on my shoulder.

"I must," I responded, "but I'll be near you even if you can't see me. When you look at the stars at night, imagine that I'm on one of them. I'll be in your heart immediately. We will see each other someday, I'm sure."

Just as my guide had explained, Daniel would be key in the mission. In a few years, as Earth entered its new level, he would be one of the spiritual leaders to guide humanity on the new path. Daniel possessed a lot of experience acquired elsewhere in the cosmos. He would apply his knowledge in his present life and would be protected somehow by the forces of nature. And I had also entrusted him to my friend.

Jensua and I left the city. As agreed, and with the authorization of the Confederation, she would accompany me on my departure to space.

We headed to the crater lake where I was picked up last time. We arrived, parked the car, and set up a tent to spend the night. Jensua was very nervous and saddened by my departure.

"I hope you come back," she said to me.

"I will always be with you," I responded. "You will hear

me, and you will communicate with me when I arrive in outer space. I hope to see you once in a while. We have a lot to do. Don't abandon Sergio; he needs plenty of support. Several people will try to harm him out of ignorance. Fortunately, he is very strong and will know how to put up with the pressure."

"I won't abandon him."

"I must tell you," I warned her, "that Sergio must not know about our extraterrestrial origin yet. Don't tell anyone. Keep it our secret."

We spent some time meditating and harmonizing our bodies. I practically did not need conditioning in order to return, but my friend did have to calm her mind, reduce her level of anxiety, and prepare herself to withstand the radiation emitted by our ships.

Towards four in the morning, I heard the commander's message. They were ready to pick me up again.

We moved away from the tent and went to the edge of the lake. An increasingly intense glow was coming from behind the mountains. Everything lit up, and daytime seemed to be all around us.

I could feel that Jensua was very nervous. Although we had already talked about all this, and she was supposedly prepared, she was very distressed. Everything she knew about me, which at times seemed fantastic to her, became real upon the appearance of the ship.

I got closer and hugged her. I surrounded her with my aura, and this calmed her down.

A ray of green light coming from the ship—now about a hundred meters above—covered us. She turned even calmer. We felt an infinite peace. We were a single being enveloped by that radiation. We kissed and wished each other luck.

I took a few steps forward and moved away from my friend. A ray of golden light coming from the ship covered me completely. My aura was now visible before her eyes. A great radiance covered me.

I began to feel lighter and started to rise.

"I love you very much, Jensua," I mentally said to her. She clearly heard these words inside her. She understood that from now on, we would be communicating this way.

I kept rising until I reached the ship. I entered it and was with my friends once more. Jensua observed us from below. We raised the vibrational level of the ship and entered the fourth dimension. She stayed there for a long time, contemplating the stars and thanking Creation for that instant. Perhaps she was taking stock of her life and everything she still had to do. She could be thinking about my warnings concerning the future of humanity and the imminent need to effect a change—the inner change every being must undertake.

Rising above the planet and observing it from its orbit, I felt connected to the whole Universe. I felt it to be a fragile being. I felt all its inhabitants. An infinite love now united me with all of them.

Today, as I write this story, I remember every moment and every situation lived next to those I love. Several months ago, I arrived on Earth as an extraterrestrial. Today, having returned to my place of origin, I feel like what I really am: a cosmic being. I feel more human than ever. We are all beings of the same Creation. We are cosmic brothers, inhabiting a universe constructed with atoms of infinite love.

Jensua and I maintain continuous communication. I know that everything is well with Zendor. Some people make fun of him; others support him. He has already written a couple of books and is leaving a deep mark on society.

"We are all interrelated," my guide tells me frequently. "That interconnection makes it possible for a small change to become a great transformation."

And I know that Zendor, like many other beings in similar activities, is making the small changes that will create the great transformation when joined together.

Several internal conflicts have taken place on Earth: climatic disturbances and natural disasters. Nevertheless, we are sure that they will soon pass and that humanity will be able to advance towards its new state. Each of us will draw their own lessons concerning what is happening and what will happen.

Today, I think about all those beings who are still alien to their true essence. This is not a message to convince the skeptical but a wake-up call for the sleeping. My wish is that their minds open up, and they find answers to their questions. I wish them all the best of luck in their individual missions as part of the global mission of helping Earth. I would like them to know that I am with them, and that all of us together are part of Creation.

I feel happy today. I am very thankful for having known Earth, this beautiful, fragile planet.

9 781777 155032